THE GHOSTS OF BETHLEHEM ASYLUM

THE GHOSTS OF
BETHLEHEM ASYLUM

Scott M. Baker

Also by Scott M. Baker

Novels
Operation Majestic
Nurse Alissa vs. the Zombies
Nurse Alissa vs. the Zombies: Escape
Nurse Alissa vs. the Zombies III: Firestorm
Nurse Alissa vs. the Zombies IV: Hunters
Nurse Alissa vs. the Zombies V: Desperate Mission
Nurse Alissa vs. the Zombies VI: Rescue
Nurse Alissa vs. the Zombies VII: On the Road
Nurse Alissa vs. the Zombies VIII: New Beginnings
Nurse Alissa vs. the Zombies IX: Calm Before the Storm
The Chronicles of Paul: A Nurse Alissa Spin-Off
The Chronicles of Paul II: Errand of Mercy
The Ghosts of Eden Hollow
The Ghosts of Salem Village
The Ghosts of the Maria Doria
Frozen World
Shattered World I: Paris
Shattered World II: Russia
Shattered World III: China
Shattered World IV: Japan
Shattered World V: Hell
The Vampire Hunters
Vampyrnomicon
Dominion
Rotter World
Rotter Nation
Rotter Apocalypse
Yeitso

Novellas
Nazi Ghouls From Space
Twilight of the Living Dead
This Is Why We Can't Have Nice Things During the Zombie Apocalypse
Dead Water

Anthologies
Cruise of the Living Dead and other Stories
Incident on Ironstone Lane and Other Horror Stories
Crossroads in the Dark V: Beyond the Borders
Rejected for Content
Roots of a Beating Heart
The Zombie Road Fan Fiction Collection
The Collector
Vlada: Tales of the Damned
Through the Aftermath: A Post-Apocalyptic Anthology

A Schattenseite Book

The Ghosts of Bethlehem Asylum
By Scott M. Baker.
Copyright © 2023. All Rights Reserved.
Print Edition
ISBN-13: 979-8-9884973-0-1

Cover Art © Warren Design

To Alina

People enter your life for a reason. As a business partner, Alina helped jump start my career. As a dear friend, she helped me make it through some rough times.

CHAPTER ONE

Bethlehem Asylum
Colorado
13 April 1951

"WHAT DID YOU do this weekend?" asked Kenneth as he and Margaret approached the dangerous patient ward.

Margaret's face beamed at the thought of her boyfriend. "Robert took me to see that new movie, *The Thing from Another World.*"

"Nikki has been begging me to take her to see it. Is it good?"

"Oh, my God, it was fantastic. I want to see it again."

"I heard it was scary."

Margaret shook her head slightly. "Not really. There were a few scenes that made me jump. I pretended to be more scared than I was. It gave me an excuse to cuddle with Dewey."

Kenneth chuckled.

"What did you and Nikki do this weekend?"

"Not much," said Kenneth. "She had morning sickness most of the weekend."

"When is the baby due?"

"About three months. The doctor says the baby is huge. He thinks it'll be about thirteen pounds at birth."

Margaret's eyes widened. "How much does Nikki weigh?"

"Just under a hundred pounds."

"The poor thing. Please, tell her I was asking about her."

"I will."

"Maybe someday Dewey and I will be doing that."

"Family life is sweet, but enjoying being single as long as you can. Once you have kids, things change dramatically."

"Okay." Margaret said it to placate Kenneth. As much as she enjoyed dating Dewey, she wanted to settle down and start a family. She had a gut sense he would be proposing to her soon. At least, she hoped so.

The pair reached the outer set of doors to the ward at the end of the fifth-floor corridor. Kenneth pressed the intercom button. A second later, a voice came over the speaker.

"Who is it?"

"Kenneth and Margaret. We're here to check on the patients."

"One second."

An irritating buzz accompanied by a metallic click echoed through the corridor. Kenneth pulled open the door, ushered Margaret inside, and followed. The door closed by itself, then the lock engaged. James looked up from his desk inside the guard booth. Nyby sat in a chair in the corner reading a copy of *Life* magazine with a picture of General Omar Bradley on the cover.

James tipped his hat at Margaret. "Evening."

She smiled. "Hello."

"How are things tonight?" asked Kenneth.

"Quiet. Thank God."

"Don't say the Q word," warned Margaret.

James seemed confused. "Why not?"

"An old nurse superstition," answered Kenneth. "If you use the Q word, it brings bad luck, and the night goes to hell."

"I don't want that to happen. Only an hour left of the shift."

"Amen to that." Kenneth stepped up to the double steel doors and paused.

James hit the button under his desk. Kenneth opened the

right door, allowed Margaret to enter the corridor, then followed. The door closed and locked behind them.

The two nurses stopped in front of the metal door to Room 11 belonging to Jacob Spencer, incarcerated for life for serial pedophilia.

Margaret shivered. "This guy gives me the creeps."

"Tell me about it. Most of the security guards are hoping he'll act up someday so they can beat the shit out of him." Kenneth unhooked the key ring from his beltloop and searched for the one to Room 11, finding it after a few seconds. He inserted it into the lock, twisted it to the left, and placed the ring back on his belt. "Let's get this over with."

When Kenneth opened the door, the revolting stench of urine and feces flowed into the corridor. Margaret felt bile rise in the back of throat.

Kenneth scrunched his face and shook his head to get rid of the disgusting odor. "What the hell happened in here?"

Jacob lay on his bed. The man was tall, standing at six feet two inches. However, being confined to bed, his limbs showed signs of atrophy. His dark hair had grown long, reaching past his shoulders, oily and straggly since he had not bathed in weeks. Margaret immediately noticed his eyes, deep brown irises that showed no emotion, only the darkness buried deep in his soul.

Leather restraints secured his wrists and ankles to the frame. Somehow, the patient had pulled his elastic waistband pants down around his thighs. The sheets beneath were soiled with excrement and urine. The waste coated his buttocks and hips. On seeing them enter, Jacob rolled back and forth on the mattress, spreading the mess even farther.

"Damn it." Kenneth's fingers balled into fists. For a second, Margaret thought he might punch Jacob.

Jacob cackled. "Have fun cleaning it up, asshole."

"I should bring in the fire hose and power wash you."

Jacob laughed sardonically. "Only if you promise to shove

the nozzle up my ass."

"I ought to—"

Margaret grabbed his arm. "Don't give him the satisfaction. Let's just clean him up."

Kenneth walked over to the bed. "Be still. We're going to take you to the showers."

"Will you wipe my ass for me?" Jacob laughed again.

"Shut up," growled Kenneth.

Margaret slid on a pair of exam gloves and pulled Jacob's pants up to his waist, then moved to the head of the bed.

"Did you enjoy that?" Jacob taunted.

"I told you to shut up." Kenneth leaned over the bed and unstrapped the restraint around Jacob's left wrist.

As Kenneth straightened up, Jacob grasped Kenneth's neck with his free hand and pulled him close. He sunk his teeth into the nurse's neck and snapped his jaws shut, then yanked his head back. A chunk of flesh tore loose, including a segment of the jugular. Streams of blood spurted through the severed artery, covering both men. Kenneth reached up to stop the flow, a useless gesture. When Jacob let Kenneth go, he fell against the mattress and slid to the floor, rapidly bleeding out.

For a moment, Margaret panicked. It was all the time Jacob needed. He reached up, clutched Margaret by the collar, and slammed her head against the metal headboard. Margaret momentarily blacked out. She tumbled against the wall and slid down, only semi-consciously aware of what happened next.

Jacob quickly undid the remaining restraint and jumped off the bed, pausing long enough to yank off one of the restraints and remove the now-dead Kenneth's key ring. Rushing into the corridor, he ducked so the guards outside could not see him through the window and wound the restraint around the handles of the twin doors. When finished, he ran down the corridor. Margaret heard the keys being inserted into the cell across the corridor and the hinges squeak open.

"Come on," Jacob whispered. "Before they know what's

going on."

The realization dawned on Margaret, and it terrified her. The inmates were orchestrating a breakout. She had to warn the guards.

Margaret pushed herself off the floor. The room spun. She stumbled, catching herself against the soiled bed. Her hand slid into a pile of feces. She ignored it, concentrating on the danger around her. Closing her eyes and taking a deep breath to steady herself, she tried a second time, making it halfway across the room before tripping. Margaret caught herself against the door jamb. Her vision and her stomach rolled. She must have a concussion. Leaning back against the jamb, she slid to the floor. When her focus returned a few seconds later, she gasped.

Jacob had already let most of the inmates out of their cells, ordering each of them to stay low, remain quiet, and congregate near the door. When he released the fifteenth and last prisoner, the psychopath named Garrett who had strangled his own mother and all seven of his siblings, they joined the others. Jacob removed the restraint from around the handles then moved over beside Margaret.

"I want you to scream." Jacob asked nicely, flashing her a friendly smile.

Margaret stuttered from terror. "N-no."

"Please." He dragged out the word like a child begging his mother for candy.

Margaret shook her head.

"Suit yourself."

Jacob lunged, placing his hands around her throat and strangling her, but not enough to completely cut off her airways. Fear overcame common sense and Margaret screamed.

Outside, James yelled, "What the hell was that?"

"I'll check it out."

The inmates huddled as close as possible to the door.

Nyby peered through the window, spotting nothing unusual

until he saw Margaret lying against the jamb. She shook her head to warn him, but it went unnoticed.

"Open the damn door," Nyby ordered.

The moment the electronic lock clicked, fourteen of the inmates surged forward, pushing open the twin doors and knocking over Nyby. Jacob removed the guard's gun from its holster and shot Nyby once in the stomach, then rushed over and pumped three rounds into James' face in the guard room as he picked up the phone and called for backup. Jacob then reached under the desk and pressed the button unlocking the outer door. One of the patients opened it a few inches so it wouldn't close.

Jacob rushed out of the guard's office. "Let's tear this place apart."

A cheer went up from the other patients and they rushed into the other wards of the institution. Margaret closed her eyes and cried, condemning herself. If she had only had the strength to remain silent, none of this would be happening. She had allowed a riot, a realization that dug into her soul as she heard their cries recede into the distance.

"Free everyone!"

"Kill! Kill! Kill!"

"We want revenge!"

A sense of uneasiness washed over Margaret. She opened her eyes and gasped. Garrett crouched in front of her, his head tilted to one side as he studied her face. He grinned when her gaze fixed on his.

"You remind me of my older sister."

Dropping to his knees, Garrett leaned forward and gently slid his hands around Margaret's neck until his thumbs rested on her Adam's apple. His fingers gently caressed her neck. Panic welled up inside of her. Garrett was going to rape her.

Margaret summoned what little courage she had left. "Wh-what do you want?"

His grin morphed into a psychotic smile. "To finish what

Jacob started."

The grip suddenly tightened. His thumbs brutally pressed down, closing off her airway. Margaret reached for Garrett's face, aiming for his eyes. He pulled her head forward and slammed it hard against the metal frame, stunning her. No longer able to fight back, she gave in, waiting for death to release her.

Margaret's last moment of consciousness was filled with the sounds of the inmates ransacking the asylum.

CHAPTER TWO

TATYANA SIGHED. "COULD you turn the TV down?"

"I won't be able to hear it." Nick sat on the sofa in front of the television, his feet propped up on the coffee table. Nostradamus curled up beside him, his back pressing against where Nick's leg would be if he were corporeal.

"Since when did you start enjoying television?"

"Ever since I realized how entertaining it is."

"You've become awfully lazy these past few months. I've never encountered a spiritual couch potato."

Nick leaned his head back to see Tatyana. "What's a couch potato?"

"It's slang for a lazy person who does nothing but sit around and watch mindless television all day."

"It's not mindless. Most of the shows I watch are educational. I've learned a lot about what happened after World War II ended. Besides, I have a lot of free time on my hands considering we haven't done an investigation in six weeks."

Tatyana leaned to the side to peer around the screen of her laptop and stared at the TV. "What are you watching?"

"*Ghost Whisperers* on the Travel Channel."

"Don't you already know enough about your kind?"

"Yes, but these guys are hilarious. They're so full of shit I'm surprised plants don't grow out of them."

Tatyana suppressed a laugh. "Where are they this episode?"

"They're in Romania touring sites associated with Vlad the Impaler. Right now, they're at his castle in Targoviste."

"Well, enjoy your show. Just keep the volume down so I can work."

"Your command is my wish." Using his limited ability to control objects, Nick decreased the volume on the television by half.

Tatyana could not blame Nick. They enjoyed hanging out together because they liked each other's company. They had not participated in a paranormal investigation in over a month ever since the nightmare aboard the *Maria Doria*. Dealing with malevolent spirits in Eden Hollow and in Salem had been bad enough. Having to attempt to purge close to a hundred enraged ghosts aboard a cruise ship with no power while caught in the middle of a Category Five hurricane proved to be the final straw. Tatyana decided to take a break from her paranormal duties for a while, finish her dissertation, and finally obtain her doctorate. With luck, she would find a teaching position soon after because the money she had saved from her previous investigations would not last long.

"That's ridiculous," Nick cried from the sofa.

"What's wrong now?"

"This idiot on TV is inside Vlad's castle trying to communicate with him in English. How many fifteenth century Romanians know English?"

"You more than anyone know that spirits can detect the presence of humans and understand what they're feeling."

"Yeah, but if some spirit asks me a question in Romanian, I'm not going to know what he's saying or be able to respond in his language. These jerks are supposedly experts in their field. These shows are all bullshit."

"Then why do you watch them?"

"It's fun to see what con artists these guys are."

"Try to enjoy yourself quietly. I have to work."

"Yes, dear."

Tatyana ignored the sarcasm and went back to writing. She got in twenty minutes of work before Nick called out, "Come on, man."

"Now what?" She made no attempt to hide the frustration in her voice.

"There was a loud noise and the three investigators screamed like a bunch of teenage girls."

"Maybe it scared them."

"Then they shouldn't be doing this for a living. I've never seen you react that way, and you've dealt with some truly evil spirits."

Tatyana could not argue with Nick about that. All the professional private investigators she knew, including herself, got involved in some terrifying situations, but never showed their fear. It gave the spirits the advantage. She had always thought most of those who appeared on national television were merely showman trying to boost their ratings. Though she would never admit that to Nick and give him the satisfaction of being right.

An hour passed. *Ghost Whisperers* ended and the channel aired a documentary about Lizzie Borden and how her old house in Fall River, Massachusetts which was supposedly haunted. The show enthralled Nick, which gave her time to finish the section she had been working on. Tatyana saved the Word document and shut down the computer, then turned on her cellphone. She had three voicemails. Tatyana listened to the messages on speaker mode. One was from her advisor asking about the progress of her dissertation. Another was from her friend Julie checking in.

Nick leaned his head back against the couch. "Do you mind keeping it down? I'm trying to watch TV."

Tatyana picked up a baseball-sized fabric chew toy from off the dining room table and tossed it at the back of his head. It sailed through Nick's spectral image, having no effect. On seeing the toy hit the floor, Nostradamus sat up. With his tail wagging furiously, he dove off the couch, scooped up the toy in his mouth, and raced back to the table. The dog dropped the toy by her feet, barked once, and begged to play. Tatyana picked up the ball and threw it across the room. Nostradamus chased after it, caught it in his mouth, and brought it back to Tatyana. She took the ball and scratched behind the dog's ears.

The third message was from Giselle DeMarco, the woman from Miami Cruise Lines who had gotten her involved in the nightmare aboard the *Maria Doria*. Giselle asked Tatyana to return her call when she had the chance. She had a request to make. At first, Tatyana almost deleted the voicemail but changed her mind. There was no harm in finding out what the woman had to say.

Tatyana called back. Giselle answered on the second ring.

"Thank you for returning my call. I wasn't sure if I'd hear from you."

"Considering what we went through, it's the least I could do."

"I appreciate it."

"What did you need?"

Giselle hesitated, as if uncertain whether to proceed. After a few seconds, she spoke.

"I received an email the other day from Daniel Knoche. He claimed he was a producing a paranormal series for The History Channel and wanted to reach out to you about being involved in the premiere episode."

"Thanks, but you know I've taken a break from doing investigations."

"I tried telling him that, but he was persistent. Rather than give him your contact info, I told Daniel I'd reach out, give you his phone number, and let you decide whether or not to contact him. He wants to have a video call with you at nine tomorrow morning. Sorry to put you in this position."

"Don't worry about it. I appreciate you not giving out my info. Give me his number."

Giselle passed along the phone number. "Are you going to call him?"

"I'm not sure yet," Tatyana said truthfully. "Feel free to tell

Daniel you passed it along, that way you're off the hook."

"I will. Thanks again."

The phone connection went dead.

Nostradamus barked. Tatyana rolled the ball across the floor, sending the dog scurrying to fetch it.

Nick hit the MUTE button on the remote. "So?"

"So what?"

"Are you going to call him?

"Probably not."

"Why?"

"I'm taking a break from doing paranormal investigations."

"But not giving it up entirely?"

Tatyana hesitated. The previous answer had revealed more about her future intentions than even she realized. She had no idea how to respond.

Nostradamus returned with the ball. Tatyana took it from him and scratched his chin.

Nick shifted on the sofa to meet Tatyana's gaze. "I'd call this guy and see what he wants. It might be interesting. And you're not committed to say yes."

"Makes sense."

"Of course, it does. I'm older than you, so I'm smarter."

"First, how old you are doesn't determine how smart you are. Second, we're both the same age."

"True. But I've been around a lot longer than you, so I'm more experienced."

"Fine, you win. I'll see what this Daniel has to say."

Nick grinned. "See, you listen to me. You're getting smarter."

Tatyana tossed the ball at Nick again. Nostradamus chased after it, jumping over the rear of the sofa. Nick chuckled and transformed into a mist that broke apart when the dog passed through it. The ball bounced off the coffee table and veered right, sending the dog scrambling to keep up.

Tatyana stood and headed for the bedroom, with Nostradamus close behind her.

CHAPTER THREE

TATYANA SAT IN front of her computer, debating whether to call Daniel. She glanced down at the clock in the corner of the screen. 8:53. Tatyana wished she had not agreed to do this but, after what had transpired on the *Maria Doria*, she could not refuse Giselle.

This call would be a colossal waste of time. Daniel probably wanted to interview her about the incident aboard the cruise ship, at Salem Village, or one of her other investigations to gather information to base a show on. Anything to increase his viewings on YouTube. What if this guy was an amateur who wanted to pick her brain on how to conduct an investigation? It did not matter. She would talk to Daniel for a few minutes then politely end the call.

Assuming the guy even answered.

The clock switched to 9:00. Tatyana sighed. Here goes nothing.

She typed in Daniel's phone number and hit the video call button.

Daniel answered on the second ring. Tatyana would not have pegged him as an influencer. He was young, mid-twenties, with better than average looks, including well-coiffured black hair and piercing brown eyes. No facial tattoos. No nose rings. No pastel-colored hair. He even wore a collared shirt. Maybe she had misjudged him.

On seeing the connection had gone through, Daniel broke out into a huge smile.

"Miss Reynolds?"

"Yes. But please call me Tatyana."

"It's so good to talk to you. It took me a month to track you down, and I wasn't sure if you'd call."

"I'm doing it as a favor for Giselle."

"I appreciate that. I read everything I could about what happened on the *Maria Doria*. You did amazing work there. But you've down amazing work on all your investigations."

"Thanks." Tatyana tried to hide her frustration. "How can I help you?"

"I don't know what Giselle told you, but I host a YouTube podcast called *Paranormal Explained*. There's five of us on the team. We do a show every two weeks in which we travel to haunted locations and conduct paranormal investigations. We've been to Lizzie Borden's house, the Stanley Hotel, the Winchester House, Gettysburg, the Tower of London, and so many more. The podcast has a following on YouTube of almost twenty-eight thousand subscribers."

"That's nice, but how do I fit into all this?"

"I've been trying to get our podcast onto television. The problem is our following is too small to compete with the other paranormal shows already on the air. There's one producer who took an interest in the podcast and is willing to give us a chance. He'll fund one episode of *Paranormal Explained* and air it on the Discovery Channel. If it gets good ratings, he'll pick us up for a year. That's where you come in. The producer feels the show has a better chance of success if we have a special guest on the premiere, someone who will attract viewers."

"And your producer recommended me."

"He left the decision to me," said Daniel. "I chose you."

"Why me? Didn't any of the other paranormal hosts want to appear on your show?"

"They might have, but you bring to the table something they can't."

"What's that?"

"You're a hot commodity."

14

Tatyana chuckled. "I didn't think I was that attractive."

"I'm not referring to your looks which the camera is going to love. Right now, you're the most talked about ghost hunter on the Internet. Every paranormal chatroom has been buzzing about you ever since word came out about what happened in Salem. The more information that comes about Salem and the cruise ship, the more in demand you are."

"And you want me to come on your show and talk about my experiences."

"I want you to accompany us on the investigation. Having you on the show with us will drive our ratings through the roof."

Great, thought Tatyana. *He wants me as window dressing.* "Thanks for the offer, but I'm—"

"Please hear me out before you say no. I've arranged for us to spend the night at Bethlehem Asylum in Colorado."

"Isn't that the institution where the patients rioted and killed members of the staff back in the 60s?"

"It was 1951, but yes."

"I thought that was closed off to the public."

"It is. My producer pulled some strings and arranged for us to spend twelve hours there. Are you interested?"

Of course, Tatyana was interested. This would be a rare opportunity to explore a haunted location with a tragic history that had never been investigated before. However, she had made a promise never again to get involved in such activities.

"I'd love to, but—"

"My producer is willing to pay you twenty thousand dollars if you accompany us."

"Are you serious?"

Daniel nodded. "Twenty thousand dollars for twelve hours of work. Any filler segments the producer asks for can be done at home. Plus, we'll pay your travel expenses. And the best part, you get to be involved in an investigation no one has ever done before. What do you say?"

Tatyana paused, mentally attempting to figure out how to pull this off. Daniel mistook it for hesitation.

"Don't give me an answer now. Think about it for twenty-four hours. You have my number. Call me when you decide. Deal?"

"Deal."

Daniel smiled. "I look forward to talking with you tomorrow."

The screen went blank as Daniel ended the call.

Tatyana leaned back in her chair and glanced down at Nostradamus. The dog raised his head and met her gaze.

"What do you think, boy? Are you interested in one more investigation?"

Nostradamus barked once and wagged his tail.

She leaned over to pet him. Then, in her best Al Pacino accent, said, "Just when I thought I was out, they pull me back in."

CHAPTER FOUR

TATYANA SPENT THE rest of the day following her set routine—working on her doctoral dissertation, taking Nostradamus for his morning and afternoon walks, then doing a few chores around the house before preparing dinner. After eating, she settled down in front of her computer to check her email and social media accounts.

Rather than watching a movie as she usually did, Tatyana called up YouTube and searched for *Paranormal Explained*. Thirty-seven episodes had been uploaded, each between one to two hours long, investigating such notable locations as the Winchester Mansion, Waverly Hills Sanitarium, and the Stanley Hotel. She scrolled through the podcasts until she came across one that piqued her interest about an investigation of paranormal activity at Captain Grant's Inn in Preston, Connecticut, only a few hours south of her. Hitting the PLAY button, Tatyana sat back and watched the show.

She was surprised at how professional Daniel's team conducted themselves. Besides Daniel, the team consisted of three men and one woman. Based on the various angles, she estimated the production crew consisted of at least two, possibly three cameramen, though it was impossible to determine whether they were permanent crew members. The equipment used was a combination of the latest, top of the line sensors and older, highly reliable gear, which impressed her.

Even more impressive was how they conducted themselves. Their demeanor, the techniques they used, and how they handled contacts with spirits seemed professional. No one overreacted if a voice came across the spirit box. No one panicked if Daniel asked a spirit to prove they were present and then something was knocked off a shelf. Most important, they did not accept every incident as proof of paranormal activity. The team seemed more interested in learning the truth than putting on a theatrical display for ratings. The opening and filler segments did have a Hollywood-style flare to them. However, they did not distract from the main cusp of the show.

This particular episode was divided into two parts, one filmed in the cemeteries behind the inn and across the road, and the other taken inside. The cemetery portion uncovered no ghostly activity despite the latter containing the grave of Adelaide Grant, the wife of William Grant, who had built the house and then was lost at sea, leaving her heartbroken and devastated.

However, once the investigation shifted inside, the spirits came out in droves. While filming in the dining room, an entity called Daniel by his name then muttered, "Kill them all," the entire event clearly picked up on camera. Upstairs in what once served as the master bedroom, someone ordered the team to get out. In the bedroom at the other end of the hall, the spirit of a young girl begged for help while an angry male entity attempted to silence her and scare away Daniel's team. Through it all, they maintained their professionalism and never once engaged in histrionics. An Internet search verified such paranormal activity was common at Captain Grant's Inn.

Tatyana looked up the team members of *Paranormal Explained*. Daniel once worked as a cameraman on three other paranormal shows before branching out on his own. Casey Weingartner was the number two investigator after Daniel. On camera, he was as professional as his boss, although she could not find any information on prior paranormal experiences. Casey was highly photogenic—tall and exceedingly handsome, with piercing blue eyes and blonde hair cut like the three bear's porridge, not too long or short but just the right length. Even more than his looks, Casey possessed intelligence and an outgoing personality that the camera loved. He fit right in.

The same could be said about Miles Landon, the youngest and most enthusiastic member of the team. Tatyana assumed him to be in his mid-twenties with above-average looks. Miles seemed most noted for the endless jokes and bad puns he made throughout the show. From what Tatyana's search revealed, Miles had no prior experience in the paranormal before joining Daniel's team. Clearly, he was included to appeal to a younger audience.

In sharp contrast stood Tanner, the more cynical member of the group. He was the most rugged looking member of the group, sporting a beard and bald head, and having spent plenty of time in the gym. Tanner's demeanor was brash and no-nonsense, clearly the team member who questioned everything and looked for ways to explain away the paranormal. According to the Internet, he had spent six years in the army and two years as a background investigator before joining *Paranormal Explained*.

And finally, Gayle Summers, the sole female member. At first, Tatyana thought Rebecca had been included because she was young and attractive, with flowing auburn hair and a firm physique that nicely filled out whatever she wore. Tatyana chastised herself when she checked out the woman's credentials. She had gotten an education from Ivy Tech Community College in Indiana on how to safely conduct investigations and properly use the equipment, had worked behind the scenes on two previous shows, and even authored a book about her experiences before teaming up with Daniel.

Tatyana had yet to determine if the team members were purposefully chosen to provide a broad array of opinions and experiences, or if it was all arranged to ensure better ratings. Not that it mattered. If the profiles she found online were accurate, this crew possessed the qualifications to make an effective paranormal investigation team.

Next, Tatyana researched Bethlehem Asylum north of Craig, Colorado. This location piqued her interest. Two photos dominated the site's homepage. The first was a photograph taken in 1908. The asylum stood five stories in height. A narrow brick structure anchored the asylum in the center with a marble staircase twenty feet wide ascending to the main entrance. Two buildings extended at a slight angle from either side of the stone structure and stretched for three hundred feet, obviously wards for the patients. Even in this antique view, the facility had a vibrance to it. The second photograph, taken in 2019, showed the asylum as it appeared today. The center structure had weathered time well, with only the marble staircase being faded and dirty. The same could not be said for the twin wards. The exterior walls had seen better days, with most of the whitewash faded and darkened and large sections of cement broken away, revealing the foundation beneath. Ironically, only a few of the windows were broken and no graffiti was visible. Considering its size, she felt certain there would be some type of paranormal activity there.

The history of the asylum confirmed that. It had been founded as Bethlehem Sanitorium in 1887 by a Mormon missionary to assist those in Colorado suffering from tuberculosis. At that time, Craig had been known as Windsor, the halfway point between Denver and Salt Lake City. A large facility was necessary considering the infection rate in urban areas was over seventy percent and the mortality rate neared eighty percent. Since Windsor was mostly ranches, it seemed the ideal location. The sanitorium quickly developed a reputation for offering comfort and excellent medical care for those in need. As the spread of tuberculosis came under control, the sanitorium found itself with more empty beds than patients. At least until 1918, when the Spanish Flu epidemic broke out and many of the region's patients were treated there.

The dark history began in 1922 following the end of the pandemic. The family of the Mormon missionary who had founded the sanitorium opted not to keep the facility open any longer and sold it to a private organization based out of Denver that refurbished the building and converted it to Bethlehem Asylum in 1925 under the control of Dr. Edmund Savage. Little information existed about the asylum for the next twenty-six years other than the trustees agreed to house the most dangerous and mentally unstable inmates from Colorado and the surrounding states. Only a handful of patients who checked into the institution were ever released.

On 13 April 1951, a Friday of all days, a riot broke out in the dangerous patient ward. A psychopath named Jacob killed a guard, stole his keys, and released the other patients from the ward. By the time the Colorado State Police entered the facility and dispersed the rioters, fifteen patients from the dangerous ward, twelve from other wards, eighteen staff members, nine guards, and Dr. Savage himself had been murdered. The Colorado Department of Health and the State Police conducted an inquiry but never released their findings. The state permanently closed Bethlehem Asylum on 3 May and dispersed the remaining patients to other facilities. The building had remained vacant since then, with no outsiders having ever been allowed inside. To prevent trespassing, the original twenty-foot-high exterior wall was outfitted with an electrified barbed wire fence.

What baffled Tatyana was that minimal information existed about Bethlehem Asylum beyond its website. Its history as a tuberculosis and Spanish Flu sanitorium was well documented. As an asylum, it received only mentions in other articles about such institutions, including a list of those located in Colorado and those with dark histories. She found some reports from several local newspapers of people who passed by the asylum and heard screams and strange noises coming from inside. For a building with such a fascinating and disturbing history, little had been published about it.

Tatyana then conducted an Internet search on Dr. Edmund Savage. She had more luck with this topic, but not by much. She found an old Curriculum Vitae from a 1950 edition of the *Rocky Mountain News*. Born in 1911 in Tampa, Florida, Edmund had been working on his doctorate in psychology at Stanford University when the Japanese attacked Pearl Harbor. Like so many other young men of his generation, he enlisted in the Army. Because of his expertise, the Pentagon opted not to send him into combat, instead keeping him at Walter Reed in Washington, D.C. to deal with the trauma of returning soldiers severely wounded in combat. Here he gained considerable insight into the minds of those who had suffered severe physical and psychological trauma. Following his release from the military, Edmund finished his doctorate and then spent two years at Danvers State Hospital, also known as Danvers State Lunatic Hospital. Following his time in Danvers, the doctor was selected as the administrator of Bethlehem Asylum.

The accompanying photograph showed a headshot of a man with a long thin face, dark hair, and a thick mustache. The cold dark eyes and lips clenched tight displayed no emotion.

No further information was available.

Having exhausted her research options, Tatyana had more questions than answers. She was also deeply intrigued by the mystery surrounding Bethlehem Asylum and wanted to know more, even if it meant undertaking another investigation.

She glanced down at Nostradamus, who lay curled up beside her chair.

"What do you think, boy? Are you up for one more investigation."

The dog looked up at her, his tail wagging, and barked.

"I knew you would be."

Tatyana took her cellphone off the desk, dialed Daniel's number, and waited. He answered on the third ring.

"This is Daniel."

"It's me, Tatyana. Count me in."

CHAPTER FIVE

One week later

TATYANA STOOD IN front of the window of her hotel room in Steamboat Springs, Colorado, enjoying the view of the Rocky Mountains in the distance. She had never been to this part of the country before, and the view impressed her. Living in New Hampshire, she was used to being surrounded by mountains. However, the White Mountains paled in comparison to the Rockies, with even the smallest of the ranges towering over those of New England.

"They're beautiful," said Nick.

Tatyana turned around. Nick lay spread out on her bed resting against the pillows. Nostradamus curled up beside him.

"Do you mind?"

"It's not like I'm in bed with you."

"Off. Now."

Nostradamus whimpered and started to get up.

"Not you, boy. You're good."

Nick smiled. "And I'm not?"

Tatyana flashed him the stink eye.

"Fine," Nick sighed. He morphed into a mist that floated over to the comfortable chair in the corner and rematerialized. "Happy now?"

"Yes."

"You know, I need to rest. I'm tired."

"Spirits don't get tired."

"I do. I spent all night at Bethlehem Asylum."

Tatyana spun around. "What did you find?"

"Let me rest a bit," he teased.

Frustrated, Tatyana pulled a container of salt from her travel bag. "Stop being an ass, or I'll lock you in the chair."

Nick became serious. "You don't want to do that."

"Is it that bad?"

"Honestly, I don't know. That place is strange."

"How so?"

"Nothing tried to contact me, but I still detected a heavy spiritual presence underlying the place."

"Good or evil?"

"It was hard to tell, but a little of both. Almost as if there were spirits that wanted to talk to me but weren't allowed to. I got that impression throughout the place."

"What should I expect?"

Nick rolled his eyes. "Inside looks like the set of a bad paranormal movie. Daniel chose the perfect setting for his show. Shots of the interior will creep out most of his viewers."

"That's encouraging."

"It's probably nothing. More than likely residue from the riot." Nick shrugged. "Not that it matters. I'll be around if you need help."

The realization suddenly hit Tatyana. "I'm not sure you should accompany me on this investigation."

"Why not?"

"The crew is going to have the EMF and voice detectors during filming. If you're there, they might pick you up and create a false positive."

"I hadn't thought of that."

"Neither did I until just now. Sorry."

"I don't like the idea of you doing this alone."

"I won't be alone. I'll have Daniel's team with me." Tatyana checked her watch. "And I have to meet them in the lobby in a few minutes."

Nick grinned. "I guess that's your polite way of saying get lost."

"At least I'm being polite," Tatyana teased back.

Nick stood and straightened his naval uniform. "Please be careful in there, just in case I'm wrong and there is something bad lurking around."

"I will. I promise." Tatyana smiled. "And thanks."

"That's what I'm here for."

Nick morphed into a mist that disappeared with a loud swoosh, which Tatyana hated. She shook her head in frustration. Nostradamus lifted his and barked.

Tatyana freshened up before heading downstairs to meet the *Paranormal Explained* crew down in the restaurant area. Out of habit, she stopped by the spare bed for her bag of crystals and salts, forgetting that she had not brought them since they were only conducting an investigation and not a cleansing. Grabbing her jacket from the closet, Tatyana opened the door to the corridor.

"Are you coming, boy?"

Nostradamus bound off the bed, ran into the corridor, and headed for the elevator where he waited for his mistress to catch up.

NINE PEOPLE WAITED in the restaurant when Tatyana and Nostradamus arrived. She recognized Daniel, Casey, Miles, Tanner, and Gayle from the YouTube show. The others she had never seen before. Two casually dressed men and a woman sat together at one table, more than likely the production crew. Another man in slacks, a dress shirt, and loafers sat backwards in a chair facing the entrance. He glanced at his watch and sighed dramatically. Judging by his pompous attitude, Tatyana assumed he must be the producer.

On seeing her, the man stood and spun the chair around. "Are you Tatyana Reynolds?"

"I am."

"You're late."

Tatyana glanced at her watch. "By four minutes."

"Time is money."

"I'm sorry, but who are you?"

The rest of the team shifted nervously in their seats.

"Joel Carbone. I'm the producer." His eyes fell on Nostradamus, who had moved up alongside Tatyana. "What's that?"

"*That* is my dog Nostradamus. He helps with my investigations. He often detects a spiritual presence before I do."

"I don't want that animal on my set."

Nostradamus quietly growled. Tatyana did not blame him. Joel was an ass. For a second, she contemplated letting her dog take a bite out of the producer but thought better of it. She did not want Nostradamus to get sick.

"Nostradamus is my pet and attends all my investigations."

Joel bristled. "Need I remind you I'm the one who is paying your salary?"

Tatyana stepped up and placed her face near his. "Need I remind you I'm the celebrity who's going to give your show the name recognition that'll make this project profitable?"

Everyone else waited for the producer's response, their gaze shifting between Tatyana and Joel to see how this confrontation would play out. Even Nostradamus stared at his mistress with uncertainty.

Joel finally softened his stance. "Sorry. I'm strung out."

"That's for sure," mumbled the female member of the production crew.

If Joel heard, he paid no attention. "My studio has a lot riding on this project. If it goes south, my job is on the line. I need to make sure we're at the asylum at three sharp so we don't miss the caretaker."

"We have plenty of time," offered Daniel.

"Better safe than sorry." Joel motioned for Tatyana to join them at the table. "You already know Daniel."

He stood and offered his hand. "It's good to finally meet

you in person."

"Likewise."

"And this is Gayle. She's Daniel's assistant."

The redhead stood and offered her hand. "Actually, I'm his boss."

Tatyana was confused. "I don't understand."

"She's my wife," explained Daniel.

Tatyana chuckled. "Now I get it."

Casey leaned across the table and offered his hand. "I'm the expendable one. When things get too hairy for Daniel, I'm the one who goes in to stir up the spirits."

"But you seem to have fun."

Casey grinned. "I do. It's awesome making first contact."

Tatyana turned to Tanner. "Is that your first or last name?"

He never offered his hand. "It doesn't matter. That's the name I go by."

She ignored him and turned to Miles, who jumped up and pumped her hand. "Miss Reynolds, it's such a pleasure to meet you."

"Please, call me Tatyana."

"I read about the incident on the *Maria Doria*. I'd love to talk to you about it."

"It'd be my pleasure."

"Save it until after we get back to the hotel," suggested Joel, anger and frustration in his tone.

Daniel led her to the next table where the others sat. He gestured toward the two men. "This is Mac and Cheese, our cameramen."

"What?"

The taller of the two men, the one with close-cropped strawberry blonde hair, grinned. "It's a nickname. My name is Stewart MacDonald." He stood and shook Tatyana's hand then pointed to the smaller guy next to him with eyeglasses and unkempt brunette hair. "This is Robert Kraft."

"I get it."

Robert waved, then pushed his eyeglasses back up his nose.

The Korean woman stood and offered her hand. "I'm Kim Hae-jin. I run the technical portions of the show, from making sure the equipment is operable and everything is recorded properly to editing once back at the studio. I pull everything together and make these guys look as good as they do. Believe me, I have my work cut out for me."

"Don't listen to her," joked Mac. "We're the artists who do all the good camera work. She merely picks our best work and splices it together."

Hae-jin extended her middle finger.

"Settle down," said Joel. "I need to brief you on the details before we hit the road."

Tatyana pulled out a chair and sat beside Daniel.

Joel made certain no one else was in the breakfast area. "I'm not sure how many of you know this, but no one has been allowed inside the asylum, except on official business, since it closed in May 1951. They made certain no tourists, journalists, or television news crews—"

Daniel sat upright in his chair. "And paranormal investigators?"

"Bingo. No one else has ever done a show here. Which is why the studio agreed to back us and pour so much money into the project. What happens in the next twenty-four hours will make you guys overnight sensations because we'll be the first to report on what's going on inside the asylum since the riot."

"And what is going on inside?" asked Tatyana.

"Your guess is as good as mine. All I know, we'll be the first ones to capture it on film."

Gayle slightly raised her hand. "Are you sure we'll pick up anything?"

"Why wouldn't we?" answered Joel. "There've been dozens of reports from people claiming to have heard screams and strange noises coming from inside."

"But nothing verified."

"That's our job, to verify and record it." Joel focused on the others around the tables. "Any questions?"

"I have one," said Tatyana. "Why has the state refused to give anyone access until now?"

"Public relations. This was one of the worst asylum riots in history. Fifty-three—"

"Fifty-five," corrected Hae-jin.

"Fifty-five people died that night. The state refused to let the tragedy be exploited."

"How did you convince them to let us in?" Tatyana already knew the answer.

Joel glared at her for a second before softening his demeanor. "There was a legislator on the Colorado General Assembly who thought it was time to make the story known so he granted us permission to film there for twelve hours."

Hae-jin frowned. "In return for his niece getting a starring role in the station's next reality show."

Joel made little attempt to contain his frustration. "*Quid pro quo*. What's wrong with that? If this show is a success, we all win. Do you have a problem with that?"

"Not as long as we record everything accurately."

"That's not an issue. I have a feeling this show is not going to lack for activity."

Tatyana noticed Daniel lower his head.

Joel checked his watch. "If there's any more questions, they'll have to wait until we get there. The caretaker is meeting us at three to let us in and won't wait around if we're late."

CHAPTER SIX

THE DRIVE TO Bethlehem Asylum took a little over an hour. Tatyana rode in the van with the production crew. Mac drove while Robert sat behind him, napping. Joel spent most of the trip in the front seat loudly talking into his cellphone. She and Hae-jin sat in the back seat, pleasantly chatting about their paranormal experiences from both sides of the camera, with Nostradamus curled up between them taking a nap. The two ladies got along quite well, so Tatyana took the risk.

"Can I ask a question about Daniel's team that might sound cynical?"

Hae-jin motioned with her head toward Joel. "I'm used to cynicism."

"Do they ever fake their experiences? You know, create signs of a presence not there for ratings?"

"No, and that's why I stay with them. Daniel's crew is one of the most reputable teams on social media, which is why their following is so big." She lowered her voice and leaned closer to be heard over Joel's tirade against someone on his staff. "The problem is, they've only investigated locations with known spiritual presences. Their subscribers love the shows because it verifies to them that those locations are legitimately haunted. Viewers tuning in for the first time don't follow us because we're relative unknowns. They prefer the more popular shows that have already been to these locations. Joel hopes that by being the first inside Bethlehem Asylum, this show will make us a household name. Well, at least with the fans of the paranormal."

"Do you think that'll happen?"

Hae-jin shrugged. "That depends on what we find there."

The two vans detoured off the road and traveled along a poorly maintained cement road lined on both sides by trees until they eventually emerged into a clearing. Joel closed his cellphone and pointed to their left. "We're here."

The two vans approached a brick wall fifteen feet high and two feet thick. Despite discoloration of the bricks and a few places where the exterior had broken away or collapsed, the wall surprisingly looked solid despite so many decades of abandonment. They continued four hundred feet and parked in front of the building.

"This is it, people." Joel opened the door and stepped out.

Tatyana and Hae-jin slid out and paused to study the asylum. It looked much larger and creepier up close than on its website. The Rocky Mountains surrounded them, their peaks hidden by a dense, dark cloud cover that had rolled into the area. The gloom provided by the weather made the asylum appear eerie.

Tatyana shrugged off a cold chill that ran down her back. "This place would make the perfect setting for a horror movie."

"I just hope it's haunted as hell," added Hae-jin. "If I have to spend a night in this creep show, I want it to be worth my time."

"I wonder how far we are from any major cities?"

"The closest city is Loveland, one hundred and thirty miles away," responded Robert as he and Mac passed by lugging a case filled with recording equipment. "The last town we passed was ten miles ago."

"That's comforting." Gayle took the end of the case carried by Mac, who also held a klieg light and a stand in his other hand.

A white van with Colorado state official plates sat by the stairwell leading to the asylum. Joel and Daniel's team were heading toward it. Tatyana quickened her pace and joined them.

A man opened the van door and climbed out. His work clothes and dirty boots immediately pegged him as a road worker. The expression on his face indicated he was not happy.

"I'm Joel." He offered his hand. "You must be Paul."

"Yup." He shook hands with no enthusiasm. "I was afraid you were going to be late."

"I didn't realize how long it would take to get here. Most of the drive is small roads with low-speed limits."

"Nobody out here obeys them. There's nothing around for miles except deer and other critters." Paul headed for the front door. "Come on."

Daniel tried to lighten the mood. "Thank you for doing this. It means a lot to us. I hope it's not too much of an inconvenience."

Paul glared at him. "It took me two and half hours to get here and will take another two and a half to get home. Then I have to do the same thing tomorrow so you can film your little TV show."

Daniel slowed down to put distance between him and Paul.

Paul climbed the stairs to the main entrance. The door was secured by three sturdy deadbolts, each locked into place with a heavy-duty padlock. He removed a key ring from his trouser pocket, unlocked each padlock and slid them into his pocket, pulled aside the deadbolts, and pushed open the door.

Joel led the way inside.

As Tatyana crossed the threshold, the cries of dozens of spirits overwhelmed her senses. A few were sadistic, one repeatedly screaming the word "kill." Most were terrified, begging for help or mercy. They all converged on her simultaneously, each vying for her attention. Tatyana had never experienced this before and desperately tried to sort through the voices. Then a powerful, terrifying entity spoke a single word: "Stop." As suddenly as it had begun, the voices ceased, and the presence of the entities disappeared. Calm settled over

Tatyana's senses.

"Are you okay?" asked Gayle.

"Did you feel that?"

"Feel what?"

Tatyana shook her head to clear it. "I'll tell you later."

Once in the receptionist lobby, Joel clapped his hands together.

"This place is perfect."

Perfect if you were filming a horror movie, thought Tatyana. The windows on either side of the door had been boarded up, the only light seeping in coming from the open door. The room looked like it did back in 1951, the only difference being that tarps covered the furniture which were buried under decades of accumulated dust. A wooden desk stood along the opposite wall and, behind it on the opposite side of the wall, the security guard station. The metal door leading into the asylum sat ajar.

Hae-jin crossed over to the desk. "We'll set up here."

Mac and Robert placed the carrier in front of it then ran out to get the rest of the equipment. The others gathered around Paul.

"There's a security bolt on the inside of the main door so you can lock yourself in. Every other door and window have been welded shut to prevent trespassing. I'll be locking the front gate when I leave."

"No problem," joked Casey. "If we have to escape, we'll climb over the outer wall."

"Good luck with that. The top of the perimeter wall is imbedded with nails and shards of broken glass. You might make it over, but you'll bleed to death before you make it to the nearest town. I've also turned off the security cameras inside the building and along the compound."

"Is that a good idea?" asked Daniel.

"Half don't work anyway. The police chief of Craig asked that I do it. The cameras operate on motion sensors. He doesn't want his people driving twenty-three miles out here for a false alarm."

"Why is this place in the middle of nowhere?" asked Gayle.

"The locals were afraid of catching tuberculosis. The only way they would agree to build this place is if it were far enough away not to be a threat."

Joel tried to reassure his people. "No problem. If we need to, we can call you or the local police."

"No, you won't. There's no cellphone or Internet reception here. You're on your own until I come back for you at six tomorrow morning."

Daniel had one. "Are there places in here we can't go?"

"Just the ward where the riot took place. It's on the fifth floor of the north wing. It wasn't cleaned up after the incident and the fire damage was never repaired. You'll know it when you see it. The door is padlocked. Any more questions?"

There were none.

"Good. I want to head home while it's still light. Good luck with whatever it is you're doing. See you in the morning."

Paul exited the lobby, got back into his van, and drove off, stopping to lock the perimeter wall's gate behind him.

Tatyana looked around for Nostradamus. He had spent the last few minutes sniffing out every piece of furniture. He walked over to the metal door leading into the asylum. He paused for several seconds, whimpered, and ran back over to his mistress.

No one else noticed.

"Come on, people," said Joel. "I want to start filming when the sun sets."

CHAPTER SEVEN

TATYANA HAD TO admit, the tech team was efficient. It took them less than an hour to set up the klieg lights around the reception desk, the recorders, and the monitors; to make certain the two hand-held night vision cameras carried by Mac and Robert functioned properly, as well as the six smaller night-vision cameras each member of the investigation team would wear on their foreheads; and to make sure everything was in sync. It might have taken less time if Joel had not been staring over Hae-jin's shoulder, constantly asking questions or giving advice until she not-so-politely told him to buzz off.

In the meantime, Daniel and his crew prepared the equipment they would use to conduct the investigation. Two of them, including Tatyana, would carry a spirit box that would detect and amplify the voices of any spiritual entities that reached out to them. The other four would carry EMF detectors that would register the electrical impulses of any entities around them. They would break off into two teams: Tatyana, Daniel, and Gayle and Casey, Miles, and Tanner, with Mac and Robert, respectively, recording the investigation. The head-mounted night-vision cameras and the equipment would remain on the entire time.

As the rest of the team prepared, Tatyana sat in one of the chairs in the waiting area. Nostradamus curled up on the floor beside her, his demeanor apprehensive. She wished she had not told Nick to join them.

Gayle broke away from the group and made her way over to Tatyana, crouching by the chair.

"What happened when you first walked in?"

"Dozens of entities tried to talk to me at once. Didn't you hear them?"

Gayle shook her head, embarrassed. "I have no ability to detect the presence of spiritual entities. I could be standing in a room full of them and would never know. None of us do. We rely on our equipment to do the detections. That's why you're here. Daniel hoped you might be able to pick up something we can't. So, what happened?"

"All those spirits talking at once overwhelmed me. Finally, a firm voice told them to stop, and they disappeared."

"That must be Jacob?"

"Who's Jacob?"

"He was a serial pedophile locked in the dangerous patient wing of the asylum. He released some of the other prisoners in that block, which is how it all began."

"How do you know this?"

Gayle motioned toward Tanner. "He's our research whiz kid. He conducted a deep dive of what few archival records exist and figured it out."

"Did he discover anything else?"

"Only that Dr. Savage, the asylum administrator, was found murdered, though the reports didn't indicate where."

As Tatyana tried to process that information, Joel's voice boomed through the room.

"We're ready to film the opening. Tatyana, Gayle, please join us."

Gayle grinned. "It's showtime."

The two women joined Daniel by the steel door leading into the asylum, which sat partially open. They positioned themselves in front of the camera. Joel stepped to their right and switched on a fog machine. A light mist flowed around their feet and lower legs.

Tatyana stared at him, aghast. "What are you doing?"

"Adding a touch of mystique to the opening."

She turned to Daniel, who seemed embarrassed. "We reluctantly agreed to the dramatic effects as long as the investigation itself maintains its integrity."

Mac positioned himself before the three investigators and aimed the camera at them. "Ready?"

Daniel nodded.

"You're on."

"Welcome to the premiere episode of *Paranormal Explained*. I'm your host, Daniel Knoche. To my right is my wife and colleague, Gayle Summers. To my left is the renowned paranormal investigator, Tatyana Reynolds, who has been involved in numerous spiritual encounters, including the recent one in Salem and aboard the haunted cruise liner the *Maria Doria*. Tonight, we're at Bethlehem Asylum in Colorado, the scene of the infamous riot in 1951 that took fifty-five lives. No one has been inside this location in over seventy years. No one knows what's waiting for us once we walk through that door."

"And... cut." Mac lowered the camera. "Do you want to do another take?"

"We're fine." Joel turned off the fog machine and approached the trio.

"We usually do two or three intros and pick the best one," said Daniel.

Joel dismissed him. "The money is in the investigation itself, so let's get moving."

BOTH TEAMS CLIMBED the central staircase to their respective investigation sites. Since there was no electricity, the investigators used flashlights to navigate their way. Casey's team exited onto the fourth floor of the north wing, one level below where the riot broke out. Daniel's team continued up to the fifth floor where the dangerous patient ward was located. Hae-jin stayed in the lobby monitoring the event with Joel overseeing everything.

Daniel stopped on the landing and grasped the door handle. "Everyone ready?"

"Let's do this," said Gayle.

Tatyana nodded.

Daniel opened the door. They stepped into the corridor and shone their flashlights around.

Mac whistled. "We couldn't have a more perfect setting if Joel arranged it himself."

The corridor stretched for several hundred feet, the beams not strong enough to reach the other end. Rooms lined both walls, the entrances spaced ten feet apart, the doors long since removed. Once painted a sterile white, the walls were darkened by years of dust and grim. Paint chips from the walls and ceiling mixed with a layer of dust covering the floors.

Gayle paused in front of one room and flashed the light around. A section of concrete had fallen from the ceiling, loosened by water damage that left corroded streaks down the wall, and creating a pile of debris in one corner. A tiny window three feet wide by one foot high sat in the top center of the exterior wall, the pane covered by a rusted grating, allowing a minimal amount of light in but preventing the patient from escaping. Due to the water damage, a musty odor permeated the walls.

"We have to film a segment in one of these," said Gayle. "Even if we don't get anything, it'd be the perfect backdrop."

"Agreed," said Daniel. "First, let's find the psycho ward."

As they continued down the corridor, their flashlights reflected off the steel door to the ward. It had definitely seen better days. Rust covered most of its surface and, in a few places, the metal had begun to flake away. The door was closed and secured by two overlapping latches held together by a corroded padlock. Daniel pulled on and twisted the lock, but it stayed closed.

"Damn." Daniel let go of the lock. "I was hoping we could

get inside."

"Do you want to record here?" asked Mac.

"Let me try something first," said Tatyana.

She stepped over to the steel door ward, with Nostradamus trailing behind her. The dog stopped ten feet away, whined once, and sat. Tatyana continued ahead. She placed her hand on the steel door and closed her eyes.

Gayle joined her a minute later. "Do you detect anything?"

"There's definitely something here. I'm picking up a subtle hum."

"Are they angry?"

"I can't tell. Whatever is here is subdued."

Gayle turned to Daniel. "We should film here. It's our best bet of picking up something."

The three investigators stood in front of the ward. Nostradamus stayed with Mac, who readied the camera. Mac gave the signal for everyone to shut off their flashlights, attach them to their belts, and readied the camera.

"You're on."

Daniel waited a few seconds. "We're here in front of the psycho ward... Wait, that sounds too harsh. Let me start over." Another pause. "We're here in front of the dangerous patient ward where the riot occurred. If there's any activity in the building, this is our best chance of detecting it."

He held up the EMF detector so the camera would catch the monitor. "Are there any spirits here?"

No response.

"Does anyone want to speak with us?"

No response.

"May I?" asked Tatyana.

"Please."

Mac shifted position so the camera would catch Tatyana and her spirit box. He nodded when ready.

"My name is Tatyana. I'm a paranormal investigator. We're not here to harm you. We only want to know if there any spirits in this building. And, if there are, do they want to talk with us."

No voice came across the speaker.

"Do either of you have anything?" she asked.

Daniel shook his head.

"Just a slight elevation in the EMF level," Gayle responded. "But that's probably nothing."

"Are there any spirits present associated with the riot?"

Tatyana increased the volume of the spirit box. The background coming across the speaker rose from a silent hum to a loud, irritating clicking.

"Please talk to me."

They waited several seconds.

"Are you getting anything on the EMF detectors?"

"Still nothing," said Daniel.

"A few minor spikes, but all within the green zone," added Gayle.

Tatyana stepped closer to the steel door and directed her attention to the ward. "We only want to help. If something's keeping you here, please let us know. We can help you move on."

Ten seconds passed with no reaction.

Gayle sighed in frustration. "This is pointless."

"Do you want me to stop filming?" asked Mac.

"Keep it going just in case." Daniel glanced at Gayle, who nodded in agreement. "We wouldn't want to miss anything."

The investigators spent the next few minutes attempting to entice any spirits to speak to them but with no success. Each took turns asking different questions or rephrasing earlier ones, always without a response.

Gayle sighed. "This is getting us nowhere."

"Tatyana, are you picking up on anything?"

"No. Sorry."

Daniel removed the two-way radio from his belt. "Casey, are you there?"

"*What's up?*"

"Are you getting anything?"

"*Just some background noise from you guys.*"

"*We're wasting valuable time here,*" Joel said over the radio, interrupting the conversation. "*I suggest moving to another spot in the building and trying again.*"

"He's right—"

"*Of course, I am.*"

Daniel continued. "Casey, you take the third floor of the south wing and two below it. We'll see if we can find anything in the central tower and the south wing."

"*Sounds like a plan. Good luck.*"

Daniel slid the radio into its holster. "Mac, stop filming, but keep the camera ready in case we run into something. We'll start with the south wing then move to the central tower. Let's go."

The team switched on their flashlights and made their way down the corridor. Nostradamus stayed behind, still seated on the floor. Tatyana called him but he refused to obey. She broke away from the others to get him.

"What's wrong, boy?"

Nostradamus stared at the steel door leading into the dangerous patient ward. She rubbed his side.

"Come with me."

Nostradamus stood, quietly growled at the door, and fell in behind Tatyana as she rejoined the others.

NINETY MINUTES LATER, everyone gathered in the lobby, tired and frustrated. Between the two teams, they had investigated all five floors of both the north and south wings as well as the central structure and came up with nothing that could remotely be associated with paranormal activity. As the investigators sat around taking a break, Hae-jin and Joel reviewed the recordings, hoping to find something they may have missed the first time around. Tatyana took a chair slightly removed from the group, spending the down time petting Nostradamus.

Casey sat cross-legged on the floor, drinking from a water bottle. "I can't believe we didn't pick up anything. Not even a false positive."

"Maybe there are no ghosts here," offered Miles.

Tanner disagreed. "No way. I can't believe a place with a history such as this doesn't have at least a few spirits still here."

Miles turned to Gayle. "How do you explain it?"

She shrugged. "Maybe the instruments are malfunctioning?"

"No way," offered Hae-jin without looking up from the monitor. "I checked everything back at the hotel. The equipment is working properly."

Joel offered his own explanation. "Maybe you aren't as good as you say you are,"

"Screw you," blurted out Daniel.

Gayle placed a gentle hand on his arm. "There has to be a rational explanation for it."

Joel moved away from the monitors and joined the others. "Whether this is or not, we can't go back empty handed. The studio will string me up."

"What do you suggest?" asked Daniel, knowing he would not like the answer.

"We have to start faking this stuff for the camera."

A wave of protests rose from the investigators.

Gayle quieted them down and turned her attention to Joel. "We told you we won't do that. We're not going to sacrifice our integrity for ratings."

"You'll do what I tell you considering it's my money paying your salaries and financing this show." Joel made no attempt to soften the threat. "Or maybe you're as full of shit as all the other shows and I fell for it."

Daniel bristled. "What are implying?"

"I'm not *implying* anything. Every investigation you've posted on YouTube has been at locations that others have examined already. I don't know if you're building off what other teams have accomplished or faking it—"

"We're not faking it." Daniel started to rise but Gayle stopped him, not wanting the confrontation to spiral out of control. "You even admitted you conducted a background check on us to make sure we were legitimate before you approached us."

"How do you explain that we're at an asylum that was the center of a major riot and you guys can't pick up a thing?"

The group became silent. Gayle looked at the others before meekly answering, "Maybe there aren't any ghosts here."

Tatyana had enough of the bickering. "There are spirits here."

Joel glared at Tatyana, shifting his rage from the team to her. "And how do you know that?"

"Unlike you, I've conducted over a hundred paranormal investigations and know what I'm talking about."

Joel's face flushed with anger, but he said nothing.

"I experienced a flood of emotions when I first entered the building that were quickly cut off. I've also sensed a background hum of spiritual activity ever since we got here. There is a spectral presence here but, for some reason, it's dormant. Nostradamus senses it as well. He was jittery when we were in front of the ward where the riot occurred."

Joel rolled his eyes. "Like the dog has any expertise with regards to ghosts."

"He's much better at sensing them than you are." Tatyana let the insult sink in before continuing. "Since we've been here, has anyone seen any wildlife?"

The others looked confused.

"What do you mean?" asked Tanner.

"This building has been abandoned for seventy years, yet we've seen no rats, mice, bats, birds, or squirrels. Doesn't that seem odd?"

"It does," says Daniel. "But I'm not following you. What does the lack of animals have to do with there being no spirits here? They're not afraid of ghosts."

"True. But they do run when danger is present."

It took a few seconds for what Tatyana indicated to sink in.

Hae-jin broke the silence. "You think there's something in the building that's scaring the animals away?"

"Yes. And it's located inside the dangerous patient ward where the riot originated." Tatyana stopped petting Nostradamus and leaned forward, resting her elbows on her knees. "If you want to talk to the spirits inside this building, we're going to have to do it from the ward."

CHAPTER EIGHT

THE INVESTIGATORS FORMED a semi-circle in front of the steel door to the dangerous patient ward. No one wanted to be the first to break in. No one wanted to be the first to say it was a bad idea.

"*What are you waiting for?*" Joel stayed in the lobby with Hae-jin.

"Won't we get in trouble for breaking into the ward?" asked Daniel.

"*There are no signs on the door stating trespassing is forbidden. Besides, Saul—*"

"*Paul,*" corrected Hae-jin.

"*Paul never said we couldn't go in there. Only that the place had been sealed off because of fire damage.*"

Daniel turned to the others. "He has a point."

"*Of course, I do.*"

Daniel turned down the volume on his two-way radio. "What do you think?"

"I say we go for it," said Mac.

Robert agreed.

"We're getting nothing out here," added Casey.

Daniel turned to Gayle. "What do you think?"

"It's risky."

"Afraid of what might be behind the door?" teased Miles.

"I'm afraid we might get into legal trouble." Gayle looked over at Tatyana. "What do you think?"

"It's not my call."

"You're part of the team," said Gayle.

"Then I say we go for it. If we're going to find anything, it'll be in there."

Tanner moved to the front of the group, clutching a crowbar in his right hand. "Let's do this."

"Break the lock but don't open it," Daniel suggested. "Mac, Robert. Don't start filming yet."

The cameramen seemed confused. "Why?"

Tatyana grinned. "Because he doesn't want recorded evidence of us breaking in."

Daniel nodded.

Tanner placed the end of the crowbar between the tackle and the bolt, maneuvered it until the metal filled the space, then twisted up and to the right. The shackle snapped free from the padlock's body. He slid the broken lock into his pocket, faced the others, and smirked.

Gayle clapped her hands together. "Everybody, get into position."

Daniel centered himself in front of the steel door, with Gayle and Tatyana on his right and left, respectively. Nostradamus stayed by his mistress. The other four stood off to the side. Each made certain their detection devices were on and, when ready, shut off their flashlights. When the team turned on their chest-mounted night vision cameras, Daniel glanced over at Mac and Robert.

"We're ready."

They lifted the cameras onto their shoulders. Mac said, "You're on."

"We're on the fifth floor of the asylum's north wing. Behind us is the steel door leading to the dangerous patient ward where the riot started. No one has been inside this area since 1951, so we have no idea what we're going to find. If we're going to encounter any paranormal activity, it'll be in here."

The two women stepped aside as Daniel pulled open the steel door.

"IT'S ABOUT TIME," mumbled Joel. He tapped Hae-jin on the arm. "Make sure you record all of this."

"I know how to do my job."

DANIEL ENTERED THE outer room of the ward, followed by Tatyana, Gayle, and the rest of the team. The area was a large room ten feet square. On the opposite wall sat the entrance to the cellblock.

The wall on their left was dominated by the guard's room, or what remained of it. The metal security door sat partially opened, its interior surface scorched. Daniel stuck his head in, removed his night vision goggles, clicked on his flashlight, and ran the beam around the room. Someone had set fire to it during the riot. Metal files cabinets and a gun safe rested along one wall, the doors open and the insides empty, the metal blackened from the flames. A few pieces of wooden furniture, including a desk and two chairs, were thrown about the room, each charred and broken. Whatever happened in here must have been an inferno. The only thing that prevented the fire from spreading was that steel plates insulated the walls of the ward.

Daniel stepped out and waved Mac over. "Mac, get some footage inside here. Robert, film the rest of the room."

Mac centered himself in the doorway and began filming. "I hate to think what the inmates did to these guards. Everything in here is torched."

"I want to investigate this later." Daniel shut off his flashlight and slid his goggles back on, then motioned over his shoulder. "Right now, let's film inside the cellblock."

Daniel studied his EMF detector. The needle hovered over the red and yellow divider. "Is anybody getting a reading?"

None of the other EMF detectors registered anything.

"Tatyana?"

She closed her eyes and concentrated.

"Anything?" whispered Gayle.

"The background hum is more prominent, but not by much. Do you want me to contact them?"

"Not yet." Daniel pointed to the door. "I want to try it in the cellblock."

Tatyana went to follow the others, pausing when Nostradamus took her cuff in his mouth and held her back. "What's wrong, boy?"

The dog released her cuff and whined, his gaze focusing between Tatyana and the cellblock. She crouched and massaged his ears. "It'll be okay."

The dog whined again.

"Stay here. I'll be right back."

The steel door to the cellblock sat ajar, hanging by the bottom hinge. Tatyana wondered how violent the outbreak must have been to have nearly ripped it off. She followed Daniel and Gayle into the corridor of the cellblock. Immediately, the background hum spiked. Something she had never felt before traveled through her senses—a feeling of dread.

"I'm getting something." Tanner moved the EMF monitor so Robert could record it. "We have a spike in activity."

"Me, too," added Gayle.

Daniel moved closer to Tatyana. "Are you picking up anything?"

"There's definitely something here, but it wants to remain quiet."

"Talk to them."

Tatyana was not sure if she wanted to engage whatever occupied this area but gave in when Daniel looked at her with pleading eyes.

"My name is Tatyana. I'm speaking to any spirits within this ward. Can you hear me?"

She felt an increase in the hum, but nothing reached out to contact her.

"I know you're here. I can sense your presence. We're not

here to disturb you. I only want to know who you are. Please talk to me."

Silence.

JOEL SIGHED AND ran his fingers through his hair. "This is a waste of time."

"Calm down. They just got there. Give them time."

"We only have a few hours."

Hae-jin shushed him. "Tatyana knows what she's doing."

DANIEL CAREFULLY MADE his way between the two camera-men. "Mac, stay on Tatyana. Robert, walk down to the other end, get some shots of the rooms, then get a long shot of us."

Robert gave his boss a thumbs up and shifted the camera down the corridor.

Tatyana waited until Daniel stopped talking before asking, "Were any of the spirits currently present here during the riot back in 1951?"

A muffled voice came across the spirit box.

"I got a spike." Gayle held up the EMF detector.

"Same here," added Miles.

Daniel moved closer. "What did the spirit say?"

"I couldn't hear it. The voice was too soft." Tatyana re-wound the recorder on the spirit box a few seconds, then replayed it. The voice was too soft to be heard.

"I wasn't able to hear your response. Please say it louder. Were any of the spirits currently present here during the riot back in 1951?'

A few seconds passed before a voice answered, just loud enough to be heard. "*Yes.*"

"Were you one of the rioters?" asked Daniel.

Tatyana brushed the question aside. "Why are you still here?

Silence.

"Are you trapped here?"

The voice hesitated before responding, "*Yes.*"

Tatyana felt a surge of negative energy. No, that was not the right word. Malevolent would be more appropriate.

Gayle became excited. "I got another spike on the EMF."

Tatyana continued. "Are you confused about what happened to you?"

No answer.

"Do you feel bound to this place?"

Still no answer.

"Is something keeping you here?"

A weird sensation tugged at Tatyana, as if the spirit wanted to answer but either could not or was afraid.

"Is something preventing you from leaving?"

The voice spoke loud enough to be clearly heard over the spirit box. "*Yes.*"

"Who is preventing you from leaving?"

A second voice came over the speaker, much louder and filled with anger.

"*Be quiet.*"

Gayle's eyes widened. "Jesus. We just surged into the red zone."

Tatyana did not need an EMF box to tell her that. She could sense two entities nearby. The first one, the one she had been talking with, now terrified. The second possessed undertones of evil. As if to confirm her assessment, Nostradamus began barking from the outer room.

"My question is to the first spirit. Is this the entity that's preventing you from leaving?"

A long pause, as if the spirit were too afraid to answer. Finally, it responded.

"*Yes.*"

The malevolent voice spoke next. "*Go.*"

Tatyana felt a surge of fear as the first spirit went dormant.

The second remained, now directing its anger at her.

"Were you telling the first spirit to go?"

"*Yes.*"

"Do you want us to go?"

No answer.

"I asked if you want us to leave."

Still no answer.

"What do you want us to do?"

"*Die.*"

The cell doors on either side of the block slammed shut, beginning with those closest to the exit and proceeding down the corridor to the other end where Robert stood filming. Fear spread across his face as the slamming doors drew closer. When the last two shut, an eerie silence descended over the cellblock.

"Are you okay?" asked Mac.

Robert exhaled and lowered the camera. "Yeah. But that nearly scared the sh—"

Something unseen grabbed Robert around the neck and lifted him toward the ceiling. He dropped the camera and grabbed his throat as if trying to dislodge something. Gagging and struggling to breathe, he thrashed about.

The others dropped their devices and ran down the corridor to help. Mac placed the camera on the floor and joined them. The camera faced the incident and still recorded.

HAE-JIN STARED AT the monitors, unable to comprehend what she witnessed. Robert hung from the ceiling as if being lynched, though no rope was visible. Fear immobilized her, a fear that threatened to boil over into full panic. Only Joel's voice brought her back to reality.

"You're recording this, right?"

"Are you serious?"

"Don't shut down the damn camera. Keep filming."

She glanced up at Joel. "A man is being murdered in there.

Help them."

"I will. I just want to make sure we're getting this."

"You're an ass." Hae-jin turned back to the monitor and gasped. For a moment, she thought something might be wrong with Mac's camera, or maybe her eyes were playing tricks on her due to fear.

To Hae-jin's horror, neither was the case.

GAYLE SWITCHED ON her flashlight and shone it on Robert. She was on the verge of panic. "What can we do?"

"Try to lift him," said Tanner. "That'll take the pressure off his neck."

Daniel and Miles each grabbed a leg and raised him up. Tatyana went to help. The moment she made body contact with Robert a wave of spiritual visions washed over her.

A hospital staff member stood in the center of the corridor, facing the onrushing patients from the psycho ward. His emotions ranged from fear for his safety to concern for the other patients in the building. He begged them to stop and not go any further. The mob ignored him. As they drew closer, he tried to block their way, but there were too many. They shoved him aside and threw him against the wall. Most continued on, screaming for vengeance. Three patients stayed behind.

Two grabbed him by the arms, dragged him into one of the rooms, and pinned him to the floor. The third, a tall man missing an eye, rolled a female patient off her bed and removed the sheets. He made a knot in one end of the sheet and wrapped the other end around the employee's neck, tying it tightly. The staff member begged to let him go, pleading that he had never hurt them, pleas that were ignored. Once the noose was secured, the one-eyed man went over and opened the exterior window. The two holding down the staff member picked him up and dragged him to the window. He fought back, stiffening his legs, but his shoes slid across the tiles.

Hoisting him up, they tossed him out the window and one-eye slammed it shut, catching the knotted end of the sheet. The sheet tightened, jerking the staff member to a stop, wrenching his neck but not killing him outright. The staff member dangled against the wall, slowly suffocating.

The image shifted to a young female nurse laying against a door jamb. Her colleague lay on the floor of the room, blood spurting from a torn artery caused by a bite to the neck. She barely noticed because a patient from the ward was in the process of strangling her. He crouched in front of her, hands tightly clasped around her throat, his thumbs crushing her Adam's apple and choking off her air supply. Lust burned in his eyes and a sardonic grin pursed his lips. Just as she was about to pass out, the madman released his grip. With a belabored gasp, she sucked in air, struggling to breathe again. The madman allowed her a few moments of solace then pushed his thumbs against her Adam's apple, this time even harder. The nurse's last conscious moment before passing on was watching her strangler laughing sadistically.

A third shift and Tatyana was in the guard room outside the cellblock. Two patients secured a guard with a bullet wound in his stomach to a chair using his belt and the laces from his shoes. Another inmate dragged in his colleague from the outer room and dropped him on the floor beside the desk. He lay in a puddle of blood from his face which had been blasted away by three bullets from a revolver. Every time the guard in the chair fought back, one of the patients punched him in the wound, sending crippling pain through his body. Once held in place, the three patients opened the drawers of the file cabinets, removed the paperwork, crunched them up, and piled them around the chair.

One of the patients rummaged through the dead guard's pockets, pulling out a lighter and laughing cruelly. Rushing over to the chair, he used it on the crumpled papers. Once they ignited, the patient clapped his hands and danced around the chair as the other two rummaged through the filing cabinets, adding anything they could find to the fire. The guard struggled to break free, stopping when one of the patients punched his wound again.

The flames rose higher, igniting the leather on the underside of the seat and licking their way up the guard's pants legs, searing away his skin. He screamed, the cries becoming more agonized as the fire slowly crawled up his body, consuming his legs and working their way up his torso. Soon, the flames licked at his face, the guard shrieking in agony as the flesh began to sear off. His cries ended when he mercifully passed out just before the fire consumed him.

A pair of hands grabbed Tatyana by the arms. She struggled to break free before the spirits could harm her. The hands held her tighter.

"Let go of me!"

"Tatyana, it's me. Gayle." She pulled Tatyana away from Robert. Once her hands left his body, the visions stopped.

Tatyana shook her head to clear her mind. When she looked up, Robert hung lifelessly in the air, his neck leaning to one side.

"Is he…?"

"Yes," answered Gayle, holding back tears.

"Take him down," said Mac.

"How?" Tanner shone his flashlight above Robert's head. "Nothing's holding him up."

Miles took a few stops toward the exit. "We have to go."

"We can't leave him," snapped Daniel.

"We can."

"No," Daniel barked. "I won't leave him."

Tatyana sensed the danger growing around them. "We have to before it's too late."

The others stared at her, disbelief changing to fear.

"Let's move." Daniel pushed them one by one toward the door.

Mac hung back. "What about Robert?"

"We'll come back for him."

As they approached the steel door to the cellblock, it slammed shut despite being dislodged from one hinge. From the other room, Nostradamus barked furiously and scratched at its exterior.

Tanner reached the door first and pushed. It would not move. He turned to the others. "Help me out."

Daniel and Casey placed their shoulders against the steel door and shoved. It still would not budge, no matter how hard they pushed. Tanner stood back and kicked it with no results.

Nostradamus' barking grew more frenzied. At the same time, Tatyana felt a dangerous spike in the spirits around her. Not anger or revenge, but violent lust.

Gayle screamed and dropped her flashlight, then shifted her body from side to side. "They're groping me."

In the other room, Nostradamus' barks mixed with angry growls.

Several hands fondled Tatyana. She sensed they were sexual predators from the dangerous patient ward. She wanted to call out for help when a spirit's hand covered her mouth. She shook away the hand.

"I call on the spirits in this room to leave us alone and return to where you came from."

Demented laughter came from the spirit boxes.

"Spirits, I demand that you leave us alone and return—"

Another hand covered her mouth, cutting off her command.

Daniel went to assist his wife as Tanner and Casey tried to help Tatyana. All three men were shoved back against the walls. When they tried to push away, something held them in place.

Nostradamus grabbed the handle of the door and tried to pull it away from the frame.

Miles heard a strange noise at his feet. He glanced down.

Three of the EMF detectors were spread across the floor, each registering impulses at the top of the scale. A loud hum came across the spirit boxes, drowning out the laughter. Suddenly, a voice came over the speakers that was loud, clear, and commanding.

"Enough."

The spiritual attack ended as quickly as it began. Tatyana's senses returned to normal with the disappearance of the spirits. The detectors and spirit boxes went silent. The steel door swung open, allowing Nostradamus to race in and rush over to his mistress. Robert's corpse collapsed onto the floor.

The team moved closer together, scanning the area for danger. Those who had not yet turned on their flashlights did so. An unsettling calm settled over the cellblock.

"Wh-what just happened?" asked Casey.

Daniel looked around nervously. "We were ganged up on by ghosts."

Gayle hugged her husband. "Is it over?"

"Yes," answered Tatyana. "That last voice scared them all away. But I don't know for how long."

"Let's get out of here while we can." Daniel made his way toward Robert's body. "Tanner, help me get him out of here. The rest of you, gather up the equipment."

Less than a minute later, they exited the ward and headed downstairs for the lobby.

CHAPTER NINE

ONCE BACK IN the lobby, the group took a few minutes to process the nightmare they had gone through. Daniel and Tanner placed Robert's body on a sofa against one wall. Gayle covered him with one of the sheets draped over an armchair. Mac sat beside his friend and silently cried. Miles paced back and forth, mumbling to himself. Tatyana leaned against the desk, trying to cleanse her mind and soul of what she had experienced. Nostradamus curled up by her, deliberately resting on her feet for physical contact.

After a few minutes, Joel broke the silence.

"What the hell happened up there?"

"Robert was killed, asshole," Mac snapped.

"I know that. I thought ghosts couldn't kill people."

"They can," said Tatyana. "I've witnessed it before."

"Jesus." Joel appeared in shock.

"Jesus had nothing to do with this," snapped Tanner. "Something evil attacked Robert and hanged him."

"More than one," said Hae-jin.

Daniel raised his head. "What do you mean?"

Hae-jin turned one of the monitors so the others could see the screen then placed the cursor over the Play button and hit it. It showed the camera view down the corridor as the cell doors slammed shut.

Miles turned and walked away. "I can't watch it again."

"What are we looking for?" asked Gayle.

"Just watch," said Hae-jin.

Several apparitions formed around Robert and lifted him in

the air. Robert began choking. The camera angle switched as Mac placed it on the floor and rushed over with the others to help their friend. Several more spirits appeared, joining the others and preventing Robert from being saved. They watched it through until his death. Hae-jin hit Pause.

"Did any of you see them?" asked Joel.

Gayle shook her head.

"That's what you captured on film?" asked Tanner. "None of that is special effects?"

"No," said Hae-jin.

"Isn't it amazing?" asked Joel.

"It's terrifying," said Daniel.

Gayle turned to Tatyana. "Did you feel their presence?"

"Not the entities attacking Robert. The moment I touched him, the spirits of several of the victims merged with me and showed me what happened to them during the riot."

"What did they show you?"

Tatyana sighed, not wanting to recall the visions. "Three patients hanged a staff member with a bed sheet, just as they did to Robert. Another inmate strangled a nurse. The two security guards outside the cellblock were murdered, one being shot three times in the face and the other tied down in a chair and set on fire."

Joel shook his head. "No wonder the authorities covered up the details."

"Did you get any other visions?" asked Gayle.

"They ended when you shook me back into this realm."

Daniel grew nervous. "Are any of the ghosts here with us now?"

Tatyana shook her head. "They disappeared when that voice screamed at them, which is fortunate for us."

Daniel faced her. "Why?"

"The spirits coming after us wanted to kill us the same way they had Robert. That voice stopped them and sent them back to wherever they reside. All I get now is the same background hum when we first arrived."

"So, what do we do now?" asked Gayle.

Miles spun around to face the group. "We get out of here while the rest of us are still alive."

"I second that," added Casey.

"We can't." Joel moved from behind the desk. "We need to find out what's going on here."

Mac jumped up from the sofa and rushed Joel. "Are you friggin' serious? Robert's dead and you want to continue filming?"

"I feel bad about know your friend's death—"

"I doubt it," snapped Mac.

Joel ignored the taunt. "We owe it to Robert to find out who killed him and why. Otherwise, he died for nothing."

"I understand where Joel is coming from," said Tanner. "But that doesn't mean he's right. We're not prepared for this. We can come back later and investigate this place. Right now, we have to get out of here while we can."

"Agreed." Daniel turned to Joel. "Call Paul and have him come get as soon as possible."

"Can we talk about this?" Joel pleaded.

"No. Call him now."

Knowing he would never win this argument, Joel removed the cellphone from his pocket and dialed. After a few seconds, he pulled it away from his ear.

"I'm not getting any signal."

"Bullshit." Daniel took the phone from the producer and checked. It showed no bars. "Dammit, he's right."

The others pulled out their phones. No one could get reception.

Tanner tossed his cellphone onto the desk. "What now?"

Gayle focused on Tatyana. "Are we safe here?"

"For now. But that's only because the spirits haven't followed us."

"Shit." Miles ran his fingers through his hair and slowly

turned in a circle. "Are you saying those things can get to us here?"

Tatyana nodded. "They can get to us anywhere in this building if they want to."

"That settles it," said Daniel. "We'll wait outside for Paul to come pick us in the morning."

"In the cold?" asked Casey.

"Would you rather wait in here?"

"No."

Gayle turned to Tatyana again. "Can the ghosts get us outside?"

"The chances are less likely. If they want us bad enough, they'll be able to reach us anywhere on the grounds."

Daniel shrugged. "Then let's hope that's not the case."

"Wait." Joel walked into the center of the group. "Let's think about this for a minute. If we can't leave here, we ought to stay and continue filming."

Mac got into Joel's face. "You don't care how many of us die as long as you get your friggin' program."

"That's not true," Joel protested.

"It is and you know it."

Joel started to say something but stopped. Mac returned to the sofa and sat by his friend.

"I thought so." Daniel clapped his hands. "Let's go, people."

"What about the equipment?" asked Hae-jin.

"Leave it for now. We'll gather it up in the morning."

As the others headed for the entrance, Nostradamus raised his head and growled. A second later, Tatyana sensed it as well. One of the spirits had joined them in the lobby. Not one of the victims. Not even one of the patients who attacked them. This one was malevolent to the extent that it scared her.

Daniel reached for the knob. The three deadbolts on the outside slid shut one by one. He pulled on the door, hoping to open it, but it would not budge. The entity had locked them in.

"What's wrong?" asked Casey.

"The door is bolted from the outside." Daniel tried it again. "I can't open it."

"Let me try." Tanner grabbed the knob, turned it, and yanked with no results. He tried it again, this time planting his left foot on the jamb for leverage, but still could not move it. After a few attempts, Tanner released his grip and turned to the others. "We're trapped."

"What about getting out through the windows?" asked Casey.

"Paul said all the other doors and windows were welded shut." Gayle pointed to the main entrance. "That's our only way out."

"Shit." Miles freaked out and paced the floor. "Shit, shit, shit, shit, shit."

Hae-jin stepped over and wrapped her arm around Miles, trying to comfort him. "We'll be fine as long as we stay here and don't piss off the ghosts."

"Are you s-sure about that?"

"Yes."

"Then if the ghosts aren't after us, why won't they let us leave?" Miles asked.

Hae-jin hesitated, looking to the others for a reasonable answer.

"They're probably just trying to intimidate us," said Gayle.

Casey chuckled. "They're doing a good job."

"What do they want from us?" asked Miles.

The spirit box came to life. For a second, the irritatingly loud clicking came across the speakers, followed a moment later by a deep voice, the same voice that had demanded the spirits in the ward to stop their attack. The voice spoke loud and clear to be heard over the background noise, speaking only two words in an ominous tone.

"Your deaths."

CHAPTER TEN

"**W**HAT ARE WE going to do now?" asked Gayle.

"You heard them." Miles bordered on the verge of a breakdown.

Tatyana moved closer to comfort him. "It'll be okay."

"Okay?" Miles yelled. "We're going to die."

Tanner spoke in a low, commanding voice. "Sit down and be quiet."

Miles stopped ranting but moved over to another part of the room to nervously pace.

"I don't want to sound like him," said Casey, motioning toward Miles, "but we're stuck between one group of spirits that wants us to know how they were murdered and another that wants us to join the club."

"There's a third set that hasn't contacted you yet."

Tatyana smiled when she heard Nick's voice behind her. She turned around to see him standing by the receptionist's desk. "What are you doing here?"

Joel raised an eyebrow. "I brought you here, remember?"

"I'm talking to a friend of mine who helps with my investigations from the afterlife."

"Great," Joel mumbled. "She's nuts."

Tatyana glared at him.

Joel refused to back down. "Is anybody getting a reading?"

Those holding the EMF detectors shook their heads, not realizing Nick did not register that way.

"Then have your *friend* knock something off the table."

Nick switched his gaze between Joel and Tatyana. "Is he

serious?"

"Do something to prove you're here."

A single word came loud and clear over both spirit boxes. "Asshole."

Gayle giggled.

Nostradamus strolled over to Nick, wagged his tail, and barked. Nick crouched and scratched the dog behind the ears. "Are you being a good boy?"

Nostradamus barked again.

"Can your friend show himself to us?" asked Tanner.

"Only to those with the ability to talk to the spirits." Tatyana switched her attention back to Nick. "What were you saying?"

"There is another set of spirits here who haven't contacted you yet. They won't even talk to me. I have a feeling that if you can get those spirits to speak to you, they might give you the answers you're looking for."

"Why won't they talk to you?"

"They want to, but they're terrified of whatever it is that threatened to kill you."

"And who threatened to kill us?"

Nick shrugged. "I don't know. He refuses to reveal himself. But every other spirit in this building avoids pissing him off, even the psychos."

"Psychos?" Tatyana asked with a hint of displeasure in her voice.

Nick frowned. "What? You're afraid of offending them?'

"Fair point."

"The spirits of the patients fear him and will do as he asks. If he tells them to come after you, you're all in trouble. One more thing. The spirit who is control here is the most malevolent one we've ever encountered."

Tatyana felt a shiver of fear creep down her spine. "Worse than Kathleen and Eliza Adams?"

"This one makes them seem like Casper the friendly ghost."

"Shit," she whispered.

"That can't be good," Daniel said to Gayle.

"It isn't." Tatyana relayed what Nick had told her. The news did not set well with the rest of the team.

Daniel spoke first. "You've cleansed locations of ghosts before. Why can't you do that now?"

"This was supposed to be an investigation. Nothing else. I didn't bring any of the things necessary to purge this place of spirits."

"Then our best course of action is to find one of these terrified spirits and get them to talk to us."

"But where?" asked Gayle.

"As far away from the psycho ward as possible," suggested Tanner. "We don't want to rile them up to attack us again."

Tatyana thought for a moment. "How about the first floor of the northern wing?"

"Why not the southern wing?" asked Hae-jin. "It's farther away."

"We can't afford to play it safe. We need to find an answer before the next attack."

"What about waiting it out until Paul comes back?" suggested Casey.

"You won't survive that long," said Nick.

Tatyana nodded. "Agreed."

"Agreed to what?" asked Joel.

She ignored him.

"Wait." Mac rose from the sofa and rejoined the group. "We need to film what happens next."

"You just chewed me out for wanting to film." Joel made no effort to hide his frustration.

"Not for the TV show. Suppose something happens and we don't make it out alive? At least the outside will know what took place here."

"Great," said Casey. "We'll become a cheap ass ghost movie."

"He's right, though." Tatyana noticed Nick nodding his approval. "Let's grab our gear and move out."

"Screw that." Miles moved away from the others. "I'm staying here where it's safe.'

"No place is safe here," said Tatyana.

"Don't matter. I'm not putting myself in harm's way again."

"Stop being a coward," barked Gayle.

"It's okay. He'll only be a hindrance to us." Tatyana turned her back on Miles, making his shame even worse. "Let's do this while we have a chance."

CHAPTER ELEVEN

ROBERT'S CAMERA HAD suffered a cracked lens during the attack in the ward, so it was left in the receptionist area, turned on and aimed at Hae-jin's workstation to record anything that might happen there. Joel and Miles stayed behind. Mac took the good camera and joined the rest of the team on the first floor of the north wing.

This would not be a typical paranormal investigation. The last time they had attempted that, the crew had lost Robert. This time they hoped to contact someone from the third group of spirits who might shed light on what was going on and do so without antagonizing those from the dangerous patient ward or the commanding malevolent spirit.

They walked along the corridor, Tatyana leading the way. Nick and Nostradamus followed on either side. She stopped halfway to the opposite end.

"Are you picking up anything?" asked Gayle.

Tatyana shook her head. "Just the same background hum when we first arrived. What about you?"

"Nothing on the EMF detectors."

"How do we proceed?" asked Daniel.

"You're in charge."

Daniel took a step back and raised his hands. "Not anymore. We're out of our league. If anyone is going to get us through this, it'll be you."

"What do we now, boss?" joked Nick.

"Shut up, Nick."

Casey chuckled. "I'm never going to get used to having a

ghost following us who we can't see."

"At least he's friendly," added Tanner.

"And lovable," joked Nick.

Tatyana rolled her eyes. "You try and contact them. It might not upset the others if one of their own reaches out to them."

Nick stepped away from the group and spoke in a subdued tone. "I'm trying to reach the spirits who remain silent and don't want to speak to the living out of fear. I've also passed on to the other side. I understand what you're going through. You have nothing to fear from us."

No response.

"These people are here to help you. If you talk to them, they might be able to set you free."

"I got a small spike in the EMP," whispered Tanner.

"Same here," added Casey.

Tatyana turned to Nick. "What about you?"

"Someone wants to talk to me, but the others are keeping that spirit from communicating."

Tatyana moved further down the corridor, trying to isolate herself. "We know you want to make us aware of something the others are trying to conceal. You can tell us."

She detected a slight fluctuation in the background noise, though it was barely discernible.

"Please, talk to us."

A garbled voice came across the spirit box.

"What did it say?" asked Tanner.

"I couldn't hear it."

Tatyana rewound the spirit box by ten seconds and played it again. The voice remained garbled. She rewound it a second time, increased the volume, and tuned out the background noise. The word came through more clearly but still unrecognizable. Tatyana rewound a third time, made further adjustments, and hit play. This time, one word came through the speakers.

"No."

"Please, we need your help." Gayle sounded scared and frustrated.

Tatyana motioned for the others to remain silent. "We're trapped in here. My friend Nick says you can help. That you *want* to help. Is that true?"

A slight pause followed by, "Yes."

"Thank you," Tatyana said with sincerity. "How can you help us?"

Again, the spirit refused to respond. Tatyana felt an increase in its anxiety.

"Is she talking to you?" Tatyana asked Nick.

"No. She's afraid to answer." Tatyana feared this would happen. "Please, will you help us?"

Silence.

"Can you help us?"

No answer.

"Will you tell us how to get out of here?"

Static.

"Can you help us get out of here?"

A pause. There was an increase in the amount of static, followed by a single mumbled word.

"No."

Tatyana tamped down her frustration. "No, you won't help? Or no, you can't help?"

More maddening silence.

"You're answer confused me. Will you help us?"

Nothing.

"Are you willing to help us?"

Still nothing.

"Can you help us?"

Silence.

"Are you able to help us?"

"This is ridiculous," mumbled Tanner.

Tatyana shushed him.

"She's screwing with us."

Tatyana glared at him.

The spirit box crackled to life and transmitted the words. "I'm not."

Tatyana waved her hand for Tanner to remain quiet. "What can you tell us?"

Silence.

"What are you able to tell us?"

No response.

"What do you want to tell us?"

The spirit box crackled. "The truth."

Tatyana glanced over at Nick. He shrugged.

"What is the truth?"

Nothing.

"Can you tell me what the truth is?"

Nothing.

"Please, tell me what the truth is."

Still nothing.

Tanner cleared his throat. Tatyana gave him a stern look for interrupting.

"What?"

"A spirit box usually picks up one or two words at a time. Don't ask questions that require a long answer."

A slight spike in the EMF indicated the spirit agreed.

Tatyana nodded. "Can you tell me where to find the truth?"

No response.

"Please, tell me. Where is the truth?"

"Shit," mumbled Nick.

"What's wrong?"

"I feel the presence of the malevolent spirit. You have a few seconds at most to get an answer."

"Where can I find the truth?'

No answer.

"Please, you need to tell me. Where can I find the truth?"

Nothing.

"Please."

Tatyana winced as the presence of the malevolent spirit flowed down the corridor toward them. The EMF meters spiked to the green zone. Nostradamus whined and moved closer to his mistress. A moment later, its voice blared from the spirit box.

"Be quiet."

The needle on the EMF detectors dropped back into the green zone and the background static on the spirit box decreased to a low crackle. Tatyana knew it was over. She felt the spirit that had been talking with her rapidly disappear. The malevolent one hung around for a few seconds. Tatyana was afraid it would attack her or one of the team members. It disappeared after a moment, leaving the corridor spiritually calm.

"Nick?"

"They're gone. He scared her away."

"Shit." Daniel ran his hand through his hair.

"Man." Casey paced back and forth. "We're screwed."

"Calm down." Gayle took charge. "Tatyana's friend said there were several spirits who wanted to talk to use. One of the others will make contact."

"They might not," disagreed Tanner. "Not after what just happened."

"Let's not panic," said Tatyana. "We'll figure a way out—"

The spirit box squawked, uttered a single whispered word, then went silent.

"Was that the female spirit?" asked Gayle.

"I think so."

"Did you catch what she said?"

Tatyana shook her head. She rewound the recording ten seconds and played it again. The voice was too quiet to hear. She rewound a second time, raised the volume, decreased the background noise, and replayed it. This time, a single word was clearly audible.

"Basement."

"Basement?" said Tatyana. "What's in the basement?"

"It's no use." Nick joined her. "She's gone."

"What's in the basement?"

Nick shrugged. "I have no idea."

"That should be easy to find out." Daniel removed the two-way radio from his pocket and keyed the talk button. "Hae-jin, are you there?"

"I'M HERE."

"*Do you get all that?*"

"Yes."

"*Good. The spirit told us we should find something we need to see in the basement. Check the floor plan and tell me what's down there, please.*"

"Hang on." Hae-jin spun her chair to face Miles. "Hand me that briefcase bag."

"Where?"

"Behind you."

"What's going on?" Joel asked.

"The spirit told Tatyana to check out the basement for the truth." Miles handed her the floor plan. She unfolded it and spread it across the table in front of her, then switched on a pocket flashlight and ran the beam along it. "So far, I don't see anything unusual. Boiler room. Generator room. Storeroom. Garbage disposal."

"*What about the basement under the south wing?*"

"Hang on." Hae-jin moved the floor plan so you could view the one for the south wing basement. "Creepier, but nothing unusual for a medical institution. "An autopsy room. A morgue. A crematorium. A medical supply clos…. Oh, Jesus."

"*What?*" asked Daniel.

"There's a room marked 'Treatment' on the basement floor of the south wing."

"*What the frig is that?*"

"Your guess is as good as mine. But it sounds like what you're looking for."

CHAPTER TWELVE

G AYLE SLOWLY SWUNG her head in a circle, using the head-mounted flashlight to illuminate the walls and floor. "This is creepy."

That's an understatement, thought Tatyana. *This place passed creepy miles ago on its way to terrifying.*

The only access they could find to the basement was a set of elevators which, of course, were inoperable. With Hae-jin's help, they discovered an emergency fire exit a few yards from the central tower and made their way into the basement. The north wing lower floor seemed like any basement in any large building—dark, dank, and damp.

Crossing over into the south wing, they entered a new realm of eerie. In this corridor were located the morgue, autopsy room, and crematorium. Tatyana picked up the residual presence of those who had passed on, a natural effect of death. The closer they got to the treatment room, the more pronounced became the underlying hum present throughout the building. Only now, it had a dark side tinged with anger, hatred, and vengeance. This entire area throbbed with potential danger. For a moment, she contemplated going back but quickly abandoned the thought, realizing they were damned either way.

Daniel stopped in front of a steel door marked with the word Treatment in faded black paint. "Is this it?"

"*Yes,*" Hae-jin answered. "*At least, according to the floor plan.*"

"How are we coming in?"

"*Audio and video are fine. Let's hope they won't be necessary. Good luck.*"

"We'll need it," Casey whispered under his breath.

Tatyana and Nick approached the door. Nostradamus stayed behind with the others.

"Are you picking up anything?" she asked.

"Nothing different than from anywhere else in here," said xx.

"Same," added xx.

"I am picking up a slightly different vibe from the spirit who directed us here."

"Anger?"

Nick shook his head. "A feeling of hope."

Tatyana turned to the others. "Are we ready?"

"No," said Daniel. "But let's get this over with.'

Tatyana pushed open the door and stepped inside.

The room looked primitive even by 1950 standards. Cinderblocks formed the four walls, each painted in a shade of hospital white that had faded over the decades. A metal stand shaped more like a reclining chair than a bed sat in the center of the room, lowered to a forty-five-degree angle. A few feet away was a small metal table on wheels. On the floor beside it sat a metal box that had suffered considerable damage, exposing its insides. Something that looked like cheap headphones had been torn out of the side and lay at a heap near the head of the reclining chair. The group went over to examine the items.

Casey crouched and shined his head-mounted flashlight onto the box, pushing it around with his hand to get a better look. It had three knobs along the bottom and a meter on top. He traced the light along a wire that ran across the floor to the wall where the plug connected to an industrial style outlet.

"What the hell is this?"

"It's an ECT box," said Tanner.

Casey stood. "A what?"

"Electroconvulsive therapy, more commonly known as

shock therapy." Tanner picked up the headphones. "These are electrodes. Doctors would attach them to a patient's temples and send electric currents through them. They're meant to change the brain's thought patterns and fight depression. That piece of wood on the table was placed in a patient's mouth to prevent them from biting off their tongue."

Gayle grimaced. "That's barbaric."

"They still use ECT today to deal with severe cases of depression or schizophrenia, or to control a patient's behavior. The methods have improved a little. Today they use anesthesia before applying the treatment."

"How do you know all this?" asked Tatyana.

"My wife had three months of ECT treatments for severe clinical depression. All it did was screw up her memory. Did nothing to help her condition. She committed suicide a year later."

"Sorry."

Tanner forced a smile. "Thanks."

Daniel circled the chair. "I assume this is what she wanted us to see."

"It is," responded Nick.

Tatyana repeated it so the others could hear.

Daniel stopped and placed his hands on the chair. "The staff here must have used this on the patients. No wonder they're angry."

Tanner disagreed. "This shouldn't have upset them. It was common practice back then."

"Then what angered them?" asked Mac.

"Let's find out." Tatyana placed the spirit box on the metal table. "Why did you bring us here?"

Nothing.

"You asked to come here for the truth. Where can we find the truth in here?"

Still nothing.

Mac began to fidget. "You don't think they suckered us

down here to repeat what happened in the ward, do you?"

"Shit, I hadn't thought of that." Tanner turned to Daniel. "Maybe we should get out of here."

Gayle agreed. "It might be a good idea."

"Is there any indication of spirits on the EMFs?" asked Tatyana.

Daniel, Gayle, and Tanner shook their heads.

"Then we stay and continue this. Let me know if it changes." She glanced over at Nick. "Warn me if things start going south."

"I got your back."

Tatyana moved beside the chair. "I'm speaking to the spirit who contacted us upstairs. We did as you asked and came to the treatment room. Where is the truth?"

Silence.

"I cannot help you if you don't help me." She took a deep breath and tamped down her frustration.

Silence.

"Where can I find the truth?"

Silence.

"It's no use," said Nick. "She's not going to talk to us."

"I agree." Tatyana stepped toward the door. "Let's get out of here."

"Wait a minute." Daniel focused on his EMF detector. "I'm getting a spike."

"Same here," added Gayle.

The spirit box crackled. "Sit."

Tatyana waved for the others to be quiet. "What did you say?"

A few seconds passed. "Sit."

She stepped over to the chair. "Sit here?"

Silence.

"Do you want me to sit here?"

A few more seconds passed. "Yes."

Tatyana turned around and sat on the rim of the reclining

chair.

"Do you think this is a good idea?" asked Nick.

"What choice do I have?"

Gayle placed a hand on Tatyana's. "Does your friend think it's a bad idea to do this?'

"Yeah."

"I agree with him."

"So do I. But it may be the only way to figure out how we can get out of here." Tatyana looked over at the rest of the team. "Make sure the camera and the detectors ae running."

"We will," said Daniel.

"Good luck." Gayle patted Tatyana's hand.

Tatyana took a deep breath, slid into the seat, and relaxed. No sooner had she settled in than the visions overwhelmed her.

Four guards brought one of the patients into the ECT room. The patient struggled and stiffened his legs, making it as difficult as possible to move him. The guards dragged him in and forced him into the reclining chair. Two strapped down the patient's arms and legs as a third secured a heavy leather belt around his waist. The fourth stood nearby holding a steel baton. The patient knew better than to fight back, though that did not stop him from verbally protesting.

"You don't have to do this to me again."

"I disagree," said a voice from behind him, the tone cold and professional. "You became even more violent after the last treatment. You tried to rape one of the nurses. I can't allow that, Jacob. You know that."

"What you're doing is inhuman."

"Inhuman?" The voice chuckled. He leaned over, his mouth moving closer to Jacob's ear. "And what do you consider the molesting of women? The physical, emotional, and psychological trauma you put them through is far worse than what you must endure. The difference is you inflict pain out of a perverse pleasure. I'm doing it to try and cure you. Relax. It'll be over soon."

Jacob began screaming profanities at those around him. The curses switched to pleas for mercy when a nurse stepped forward and slid a pair of electrodes onto his temples, holding them in place with a tight headband. As she moved away, Jacob resumed the cussing. Two of the guards stepped up, one holding open Jacob's mouth while the other put into place the wooden mouth guard.

The man who had been taunting Jacob came into view. He wore a long, white doctor's coat. The doctor was tall and lanky, with a long face, dark hair, a thick mustache, and cold dark eyes. Ignoring Jacob, the man walked over to the ECT machine on the table and spoke to the nurse standing by it.

"Turn it on."

The nurse reached down and set the power switch into the ON position. An electrical whir filled the room and the main power light glowed white. The security guards stepped back a few feet. The doctor turned to face Jacob, massaging his chin with his right hand as he contemplated.

"Set the dial to two hundred volts."

She studied him for a second. "Are you sure?"

The man repeated his command, his tone quiet but forceful. "Set the dosage to two hundred volts."

The nurse did as she was told.

"Don't do this," warned Jacob, his tone having switched from fear to anger.

"Administer a five second treatment."

"No!" yelled Jacob.

His scream was cut off when two hundred volts of electricity shot through Jacob's brain. With no anesthesia, his body convulsed violently, his limbs and head banging against the chair despite the restraints. Wet spots stained his pants as he urinated and soiled himself. After what seemed like an eternity, the current stopped. Jacob's body relaxed, though his lungs gasped for air.

The doctor gazed at Jacob, his expression lacking any emotion.

"Administer another five second treatment."

Jacob did not have enough energy to cry out. When the current flowed through him, his body stiffened again. His left leg slammed against the metal frame, fracturing the tibia and breaking the fibula. The pain from the break overwhelmed Jacob and he fell unconscious.

The scene switched from the treatment room to one the cellblocks of the dangerous patient ward. A man in his early twenties, but who appeared ten years older, sat on his bed in the corner of the cell wearing only a knee-length gown made of course material. Tatyana could read his mind. The patient had a history of uncontrollable violence, having raped and mutilated several women before his eventual arrest and confinement to Bethlehem. On his third day here, he attacked a nurse and attempted to assault her, only to be beaten down so severely by several guards that he had to be transferred to the infirmary. While there, he stole a scalpel, cut off his penis to prevent himself from further sexual indulgences, then used the instrument to slice the throat of one of the nurses. Five guards were required to subdue him, one having his ear bitten off in the struggle. From then on, drastic measures were implemented to restrain the prisoner.

A steel pole six feet in height had been imbedded into the floor directly behind the headboard. An iron ring had been welded around his neck and attached to the central portion of the pole with a chain eighteen inches long. An iron bar tightly circled his waist, also attached to the pole by an eighteen-inch chain, while a second bar two inches thick wrapped around his arms, pinning them to his side. The patient had limited mobility, barely allowing him to lay down or sit upright in bed.

The guards would check in on him three times a day, once in the morning and early evening to feed him, and again in the afternoon to wash him down with a hose. Urine and feces covered his lower body for a good part of the day, causing rashes and open sores that became infected. The mattress and gown were only changed once a week, meaning the patient had to spend most of his time in material drenched with water. He had lost several teeth and was partially blind in one eye from the beatings he received every time he acted up during the guards' visits.

A third image flooded Tatyana's mind. This one of a young woman sixteen years old strapped into a hospital bed, although the restraints were not necessary. She had been heavily sedated to calm her schizophrenia-related insomnia, the dosage used so high it kept her in a constant drug-induced coma. However, the drug they used only numbed her bodily functions but not her mind, a condition which, under the circumstances, proved terrifying.

Two male nurses and a security guard snuck into her room, the latter scanning the corridor to make certain no one had seen them enter. Not that anyone would. It was the middle of the night shift, and two nurses were the only ones working the entire floor. The teenager braced herself, knowing what would happen next.

As they approached the bed, the guard stayed back a few feet. "Are you sure about this?"

"No problem," said the tall blonde male nurse.

"We do it all the time," added the shorter male nurse with dark hair.

"I don't know." The guard glanced back over to the door. "What if we get caught?"

"We're the ones who would catch you. You're safe."

"We're willing to share," said the taller man. "If you're afraid, you can back out. But you better keep this to yourself."

The guard threw up his hands. "I'm in."

"Good." The dark-haired nurse patted him on the shoulder. "We'll even let you go first."

The guard cautiously approached the bed then hesitated.

"Go ahead," urged the blonde man.

The guard stepped over to the bed and pulled the teenager's hospital gown up around her waist. She would have winced if she had control over her muscles. Instead, she merely lay there.

The guard unbuckled his belt, unzipped his trousers, and dropped them around his ankles. "Are you going to watch?"

The two nurses laughed.

"Of course," said the blonde. "That's part of the fun."

"Go ahead," urged the dark-haired nurse. "We'll let you watch us."

The guard got into bed and crawled on top of her. For the next fifteen minutes, she lay motionless, being used by these three men who treated her with no dignity. Though her body could not feel the physical effects of the violation, she still experienced the emotional trauma—the fear, humiliation, guilt, and self-loathing. And worse, the certainty that this would happen tomorrow.

Tatyana was yanked out of this nightmare image and thrown into another. A young woman in her early twenties sat in the corner of a padded room, a straitjacket holding her arms in place. Somehow, Tatyana knew her name was Sandra. Suffering from manic-depressive disorder, she often went from docile and pleasant to violent and angry. Her last outburst twenty-four hours ago had been the final straw for her attending psychiatrist. Bound and drugged, she had been placed in this cell and left unattended until she cooled off. The sedatives not only calmed her violent behavior, but they also relaxed her muscles. Being eight and a half months pregnant, the young woman had delivered her child, alone and disabled. She now stared between her spread legs at a pool of blood and placenta and, in the middle of it, her stillborn baby.

The woman suddenly looked up, making eye contact with Tatyana despite this being only a spiritual apparition. Her eyes were flushed and red from crying. Tears had long since dried on her cheeks. She sobbed once. Her lips quivered. When she spoke, Tatyana recognized it as the same voice that urged them to come to the treatment room.

"I never even had the chance to name her."

Tatyana was dramatically snapped back to the present, swaying from dizziness. Tanner and Casey each grabbed an arm and steadied her.

"Are you okay?" Gayle asked.

Tatyana gasped and tried to steady herself. Before she could answer, Nostradamus' ears went flat, and he began growling.

"Shit," said Nick.

"What's wrong?" asked Mac.

"Those spirits that attacked you in the ward are on their way here."

Tatyana relayed the information.

"Let's move," ordered Daniel.

The team headed for the exit. Gayle and Mac entered the corridor.

MILES STARED AT the monitor. His eyes went wide in disbelief. "What the hell is that?"

Fifteen spectral images floated down the corridor, rapidly closing in on the treatment room.

"Should we warn them?" asked Joel.

Hae-jin shook her head. "It's too late."

TANNER WAS ABOUT to join the others in the corridor when something spectral grabbed his arms and threw him onto the floor. Daniel and Casey went to help him but were shoved against the wall by four other spirits that held them in place.

Tanner tried to stand. He was pulled off the floor, dragged across the room, and thrust into the reclining chair. He struggled to get up, but spectral hands held him in place. One by one, the straps wrapped around his wrists and ankles. The harder Tanner fought, the more violent became the efforts to hold him in place. Once his limbs were secured, the spirits placed the final strap across his chest and yanked tight, causing Tanner to wince.

"Get me out of here."

Daniel and Casey were still held against the wall. Mac placed the camera on the floor and ran back in to help, only to be shoved against the opposite wall. Gayle was held in place, her arms pinned to her sides.

Tatyana tried to rush over to help. Although the spirits did not manhandle her as they did the others, they blocked her, preventing her from going to Tanner's assistance. Nostradamus moved up alongside his mistress, growling at the unseen assailants.

The electrodes levitated off the floor and slid over Tanner's temples. He violently shook his head to prevent it from happening to no avail. A leather band slipped over his temples and tightened, holding the electrodes in place.

The usually calm Tanner panicked. "Come on, guys. Get me out of here."

"They won't let us move," said Daniel.

The power switch on the ECT machine moved to ON. The machine buzzed as electricity flowed through it and the main power light glowed white.

"How is that thing working without electricity?" asked Tatyana.

"They're siphoning power from the beyond," Nick explained.

The hum slowly grew louder as the spirits turned the power dial to its highest setting—two hundred and fifty volts.

"Screw you, man." Tanner said it to no one in particular. "I'm not scared—"

The treatment button pressed. An intense electric shock coursed through Tanner. He cried out as his body stiffened and his limbs convulsed. The shock lasted five seconds before subsiding. Tanner moaned and rolled his head from side to side. He tried to get up but collapsed back into the chair. Turning his head to the others, he croaked out the word, "Help."

The others tried to assist him, but the spirits restrained them.

"I address myself to the purest entities of the spiritual world," said Tatyana. "I ask you to grant me the power to overcome fear and darkness. Forgive my sins and imperfections, cleanse my soul, and imbue me with the ability to confront and defeat the vile entities before me. By all that is good and holy, I bow in humility before you and ask that you cover me with the white light and protection of purity. I claim the protection of this light for myself, for my friends, and for all those in this building. I stand against all that is evil and negative. In the name of the purest entities of the spiritual world, I command that the entities in this room move on to the afterlife and leave us alone."

Several of the spirits laughed, their taunts eerily audible within the confines of the room.

"In the name of the purest entities of the spiritual world, I demand that the entities in this room move on to the afterlife and leave us alone."

The hum of the ECT machine grew louder.

"No!" Tatyana rushed to help Tanner, only to be shoved across the room and pinned against the wall. Nostradamus ran over to his mistress, frustrated by his inability to ward off her assailants.

The treatment button pressed a second time, sending another bolt of electricity through Tanner. This time, the torture lasted for more than ten seconds before the spirits relented. Tanner groaned as his body convulsed again under the shock. His jaw slammed tight, breaking several of his teeth which dropped to the back of his throat, causing him to gag. He lost control of his bowels and bladder. When the flow of electricity finally subsided, Tanner lay slumped in the chair, the only signs of life being his heavy breathing and the quivering of his lips.

Gayle sobbed. Mac fell to his knees and vomited.

Nick approached the spirit standing by the ECT machine, the one with the twisted leg.

"Stop this."

The spirit turned to him. "Why?"

"He doesn't deserve this."

"Neither did we." The spirit glared at Nick, his insanity and anger boiling to the surface. "Yet that didn't prevent the staff from torturing us."

"So, you want revenge."

"Yes," several of them shouted.

"But this man did nothing to harm you."

"It doesn't matter. We've suffered too long. Now it's our chance to return the indignity."

While still focusing his gaze on Nick, the spirit pressed the button again, sending a third charge of electricity through Tanner and allowing the current to flow continuously. This time, Tanner screamed. His body convulsed violently, the right leg slamming so violently against the metal frame that it fractured. After fifteen seconds, he began foaming at the mouth and blood dripped from his nostrils. Tanner's skin turned red as his body temperature climbed. At several spots along his arms and chest, the underlying tissue swelled, pushing against the outer layer of skin until Tatyana thought it might burst open. After twenty seconds, Tanner's chest heaved, and his body went limp. After twenty-three seconds, smoke rose from Tanner's skull accompanied by a sound that resembled bacon sizzling in a skillet. The odor of smoked flesh infiltrated the room.

"Turn it off!" screamed Gayle.

The spirit kept the device running for another ten seconds before the doctor's voice uttered a single word.

"Enough."

The crippled spirit shut down the ECT device and disappeared, along with the others in the room. With the spectral presences gone, the team was able to move freely again.

Tanner lay lifeless in the reclining chair, a small plume of white smoke rising from his skull. Gayle rushed over and held his cheek. Tanner's skin was excessively warm from his electrocution.

Daniel grabbed Tanner's wrist and checked his pulse. "He's gone."

Tears flowed down Gayle's cheeks.

"Let's bring him upstairs with Robert," suggested Mac.

Daniel and Casey began unstrapping Tanner from the chair when Tatyana's spirit box came to life. A single command came over the speakers.

"Leave."

"Not until we get our friend," said Daniel.

"Now!"

Tatyana sensed a dangerous spike in the malevolence of the spirit. She realized the danger they faced, and it terrified her.

"Don't argue with him," she told the others. "Let's go."

"What about Tanner?" asked Daniel.

"We can come back for him later."

"No," protested Gayle.

Tatyana fixed her gaze on Gayle, her eyes warning the woman not to argue. "If we don't get out of here now there may not be a later."

The others did not hesitate. One by one, they ran out into the corridor. Mac paused long enough to pick up the camera. Tatyana, Nick, and Nostradamus were the last ones out. As the three entered the corridor, they sensed the malevolence quiet down.

"We're safe," said Nick.

"Yeah," said Tatyana. "But for how long?"

CHAPTER THIRTEEN

W HEN THE TEAM arrived back at the lobby, they were clearly shaken. Joel stared at them in a near state of shock. Miles leaned against the wall, bordering on a complete nervous breakdown. Even Hae-jin seemed rattled by what she had witnessed. The three stared at the others as they entered.

Gayle collapsed into a chair, with Daniel sitting on the arm to comfort her. Casey wandered off into one of the corners and slouched against the wall, needing a few moments to himself. Mac silently handed the camera to Hae-jin before going over to sit on the edge of the sofa by Robert's body. Tatyana entered last along with Nick and Nostradamus.

"What happened down there?" asked Joel.

Daniel glanced over at him. "Didn't you see it on the video feed?"

"We did," answered Hae-jin. "We still can't believe what we witnessed."

"Believe it." Casey stayed in the corner. "It was worse than when we were attacked in the psycho ward."

Hae-jin shifted her gaze to Tatyana. "What was going on while you were in the chair. Your body convulsed, but you didn't seem scared or in pain."

"I wasn't."

"And the area blurred as if spirits enclosed you."

"They did."

"What happened?" asked Joel.

"They wanted to show me something."

Tatyana spent the next several minutes describing the

events the spirits had shown her, from the brutal ECT treatment to the death of the neglected infant, sparing no details. When she finished, the others were speechless. A stunned silence settled over the lobby.

Joel spoke first. "Can you trust what the ghosts showed you?"

"Why would the spirits lie to her?" asked Gayle.

"Because they're psychos. They can't be trusted."

Miles shook his head. "Keep talking like that and you'll get us all killed."

"That's enough," barked Tatyana, ending any further arguments. "And yes, they were relating the truth. Or at least the truth as they perceived it. When the spirits contact me, I experience the same emotions as them, whether it's fear, anger, hatred, or something else. We were led down to that room specifically so those spirits that were afraid to reach out to us elsewhere could have the chance to tell their side of the story. Bethlehem is famous for the riot that took place. Its dark history has never been revealed until tonight."

"Do you think that's why the state closed this place and sealed all the documents?" asked Daniel.

"I'm convinced of it."

"I'm confused." Hae-jin rubbed her eyes. "Why didn't these ghosts reach out to you earlier? God knows I hate to admit Joel might be right…"

Joel extended his middle finger.

"… but why not tell us up front? Why all the secrecy?"

"Because they're scared."

"They're terrified," added Nick, though no one other than Tatyana could hear him.

"Of the ghosts that attacked us?" asked Gayle.

"No." Tatyana leaned against the wall. "Those spirits can't harm the ones that talked to me. They're afraid of the one entity that has full control over this place."

Daniel shifted on the arm of the chair to face Tatyana. "Is

that the spirit that called off the attack on us after Robert was killed?"

"Yes. I got a brief glimpse of him in one of the spectral flashbacks. He looked familiar, but at the time I didn't recognize him. I was too busy absorbing everything the spirits were throwing at me. Now I can place a name to the face."

"Who is it?" asked Joel.

"Dr. Savage, the head of the institution."

"Shit," mumbled Miles. "We're screwed."

"Knock it off," said Daniel. Then, to Tatyana, "How do you know it's Dr. Savage?"

"I research all my cases before I take them. His was the only name I found associated with this place. I recognized the doctor from his photo in the newspapers. He's the one who commands the rioters when they attack us, and he's the one who calls them off. They obey him not because they want to, but because they're also terrified of him. It's the same fear that keeps the less violent spirits quiet."

"Wait a minute. Let me get this straight." Joel paced back and forth behind the reception desk as he gathered his thoughts. "You're suggesting the psychos didn't start the riot because they were nutjobs. They were protesting the way they had been mistreated?"

"Protesting is a bit of an understatement, but yes.

"Friggin' great." Miles pushed himself off the wall and approached the others. "They're out for revenge."

"Yes."

Miles seemed awestruck. "So, the rioters are actually the good guys?"

"I wouldn't go that far," said Tatyana. "The rioters had a legitimate reason for what they did but killed a lot of innocent people in the process. The real evil in this place is Dr. Savage."

"How did the doctor die?" asked Hae-jin.

Tatyana shrugged. "I don't know. The reports on the deaths of the patients and staff were never released. Based on what the spirits are telling me, their deaths must have been violent."

"Do we know what happened to Dr. Savage?" asked Gayle. "Or where he died?"

"I think I can answer that last one." Nick moved closer to Tatyana. "I'm picking up the doctor's presence on the top floor above us."

Tatyana turned to Hae-jin. "What's on the top floor?"

"Hang on a second." She thumbed through the floor plans.

Daniel seemed confused. "Why do you want to know what's above us?"

"Nick says he's picking up the doctor's presence on the top floor."

"Your ghost friend giving you advice again?" mocked Joel.

"He knows more about this subject than you do."

Joel was about to reply when Hae-jin called out, "I got it."

Tatyana moved around to her position and they both studied the floor plan.

Hae-jin whistled between her teeth. "That's not good."

Miles spun around. "What's not good?"

Tatyana looked up from the plans. "Doctor Savage's office suite is located on the top floor."

CHAPTER FOURTEEN

THE GROUP CAUTIOUSLY made their way up the stairwell to the fifth floor, with Tatyana and Nostradamus leading the way. Mac followed behind and to her right, filming the entire time, while Daniel stayed to her left, holding the spirit box. Gayle and Casey came next, each holding an EMF detector. Joel brought up the rear. Hae-jin stayed behind monitoring events with Miles. Each of them experienced a sense of foreboding over what would happen in the next few minutes, especially since their last two encounters did not go so well.

A single small window installed halfway up the wall on each landing provided little light, forcing them to use their head-mounted flashlights.

"Are you picking up anything?" asked Tatyana.

"Nothing," said Casey.

"Same here," added Gayle. "What about you?"

"That background hum is getting more intense but, other than that, nothing."

Joel cleared his throat. "Do you think it's a good idea for all of us to be here?"

"Yes." Daniel glanced over his shoulder at the producer. "If something happens, we'll need everyone we have to get us out."

"But is it a good—"

Gayle stopped and spun around. Joel stopped short to prevent himself from running into her.

"Quit whining. You're in as much danger as the rest of us, so man up and take the same risks."

She turned and followed the others, leaving a chastised Joel behind.

Nick waited outside the door to the office suite as the group arrived at the fifth-floor landing.

"What took you so long?" he asked, trying to break the tension.

Tatyana ignored him. "Is the doctor in there?"

"Something is, but I can't tell what. Its presence is strong, but it's not emitting any indication of fear, anger, or malevolence."

She mouthed the word "thanks" and turned to the others. "Is everyone ready?"

Daniel nodded. "Let's do this."

Tatyana opened the door to the office suite and pushed it open.

The outer office was a shambles. The chairs and sofa were overturned, their leather coverings slashed repeatedly and much of the stuffing pulled out. Every lamp and every wall hanging, including the doctor's diplomas, had been smashed. The secretary's desk had been shoved into one corner at an awkward angle and everything on top shoved off and scattered across the floor. Riverlets of dried blood stained the wooden surface and ran down the sides, with some sprayed along the wallpaper.

Gayle stood in the center of the room, watching the needle on her EMF detector. "I'm picking up something. The needle is hovering in the center of the yellow zone."

Casey walked over to the desk. The needle on his detector swung into the red zone. "It's stronger over here."

Tatyana moved over and placed her hand on the desk. Images from that horrifying night flashed through her mind. The secretary, an attractive middle-aged woman with her blonde hair tied up in a bun, heard the approaching mob and rushed over to the main entrance to bolt the door. The mob burst through before she had a chance to secure it. Most headed for the doctor's office. Three of the patients grabbed the secretary, dragged her over to the desk, cleared the top, and threw her on it. The terrified woman screamed and desperately fought back as her attackers tore off her clothes and proceeded to rape her, two pinning her down while the third had his way, then switching out. When finished, one of the patients with a sadistic gleam in his eyes picked up the letter opener from off the floor and stabbed the poor woman so many times Tatyana lost count. Blood spurted from an artery that had been severed, splashing up along the wall. The rest pooled on her body, overflowed onto the desk, and ran down the sides. A wave of nausea hit Tatyana at the intensity of the image. She quickly removed her hand and backed away.

Daniel raised the spirit box closer to his ear so he could hear any responses. "Is the spirit who was killed in this room—"

Tatyana placed her hand on the box and lowered it. "Don't do that."

"Why?"

"Trust me, you don't want to know what happened in here."

From in front of the door opposite the main entrance, Nick caught Tatyana's attention. "This was Dr. Savage's office."

Tatyana stepped over, grabbed the knob, took a deep breath to steady her nerves, and entered.

Savage's office was spacious and, at least before the riot, elegantly decorated. A large bay window on the opposite wall overlooking the front of the asylum allowed moonlight to filter through, which gave the office an eerie appearance. A mahogany desk sat in front of the bay window but, unlike the one in the secretary's office, seemed untouched. The rest of the furniture in the room was pushed around but not destroyed. The only signs of violence came from a Maria Theresa chandelier that had been yanked out of the ceiling and now lay shattered on the expensive Persian rug that sat in the center of the room.

Daniel looked around, shining his flashlight into all corners of the room. "I'm surprised."

"About what?" asked Gayle.

"This room doesn't have as much damage as the outer office. I assumed the patients would have slaughtered the doctor if they caught him in here."

"What about electronic readings?" asked Tatyana.

The other members checked their devices. Nothing.

"Maybe they caught him somewhere else," said Gayle. She turned to Tatyana. "Did any of the records indicate where they found the doctor's body or what happened to him?"

"No."

"What do we do now?" asked Joel.

Tatyana made her way over to the desk and stood behind it, her back to the window. The light coming through cast eerie shadows through the office. Nostradamus followed her. Knowing what his mistress was about to do, he whimpered, begging her not to go through with it. Tatyana scratched him behind the ears.

"The only thing to do now is let the good doctor tell his side of the story."

"You know this is extremely dangerous?" asked Nick.

"What choice do we have?" Then, to the rest of the team, "Make sure you record everything from here on."

"I will," said Mac.

"Good luck," added Gayle.

Tatyana placed the spirit box on top of the desk and sat down. Taking a deep breath, she placed her hands on the surface.

Her spirit was immediately transported back in time.

Dr. Savage stood at the podium. Highly intelligent and with a confidence that bordered on arrogance, he lectured to a college auditorium half-filled with students. Those attending had expressions ranging from fascination to confusion to outright disdain.

"Insanity cannot be cured. Once the mind is distorted in that way, a medical solution to the problem is impossible. The condition is the result of vitiated judgement. Those who suffer from the condition will never be cured by drugs or medical procedures. However, they do respond to coercion, restraints, and physical treatments and, as such, can be trained to behave acceptably so they no longer must be confined to cells in the dangerous patient ward."

"Trained?" asked a young man in the front row. "These patients are humans, not animals. How can you even contemplate treating them in this manner?"

"My manner of treatment is quite humane. An animal that is suffering from distemper would be put down without a second thought. Rather than throwing them into a prison cell for the rest of their lives, my method at least gives them a chance to live a relatively normal life within the confines of the institution."

"But these people are suffering from a medical condition, much like cancer or diabetes, and can be cured."

"I disagree. Mental instability and psychological disturbances are not something one can catch like a virus or bacteria. These are inherently innate parts of the human condition. You cannot treat mental disorders with medicines any more than can treat autism. At best, drugs only conceal the symptoms. After a while, the patient's body becomes used to the treatment options, much like an alcoholic builds a tolerance to liquor, and requires either a larger dosage or a stronger medication. It's the same as treating skin cancer with cosmetics. No, the only way to properly deal with those suffering from mental and psychological disorders is aversion therapy."

The image shifted to the one she had earlier of Jacob receiving an ECT treatment, only this time from the doctor's perspective. Four guards brought Jacob into the ECT room and forced him into the reclining chair.

"You don't have to do this to me again."

"I disagree," said a voice from behind him, the tone cold and professional. "You became even more violent after the last treatment. You tried to rape one of the nurses. I can't allow that, Jacob. You know that."

"What you're doing is inhuman."

"Inhuman?" The doctor chuckled. He leaned over, his mouth moving closer to Jacob's ear. "And what do you consider the molesting of women? The physical, emotional, and psychological trauma you put them through is far worse than what you must endure. The difference is you inflict pain out of a perverse pleasure. I'm doing it to try and cure you. Relax. It'll be over soon."

Jacob began screaming profanities at those around him. The curses switched to pleas for mercy when a nurse stepped forward and slid a pair of electrodes on his temples, securing them in place with a tight headband. As she moved away, Jacob resumed the cussing. Two of the guards stepped up, one holding open Jacob's mouth while the other put into place the wooden mouth guard.

Dr. Savage walked over to the ECT machine on the table and spoke to the nurse. "Turn it on."

The nurse reached down and set the power switch to the ON position. An electrical whir filled the room and the white power light glowed. The security guards stepped back several feet.

"Set the dosage to two hundred volts."

She studied him for a second. "Are you sure?"

"Set the dosage to two hundred volts."

The nurse obeyed.

"Don't do this," warned Jacob.

"Administer a five second treatment."

"No!" yelled Jacob.

The scream was cut off when two hundred volts of electricity shot through Jacob's brain. His body convulsed violently, his limbs and head banging against the chair despite the restraints.

The current stopped. Jacob's body relaxed, though his lungs gasped for air.

"Administer another five second treatment."

When the current flowed through Jacob, his body stiffened again. His left leg banged against the metal frame of the chair, fracturing the tibia and breaking the fibula. The pain from the fracture overwhelmed Jacob and he fell unconscious.

"That's enough," ordered the doctor. He stepped over and patted Jacob on the shoulder. "Hopefully, this time the treatment will have cured your anger."

As the nurse removed the electrodes and the guards dragged Jacob's limp body back to his cell, Dr. Savage stepped over to the counter against the wall and took extensive notes on the treatment administered to the patient.

The image switched to the doctor's office. He sat in his chair, listening to the alarm bell ringing and the distant carnage in the corridors of the north wing. A knock came on the door. He knew it must be Amelia, his secretary. The patients would not have shown such niceties.

"Come in."

Amelia stepped inside and stopped after a few steps. Her eyes were wide with fear and her hands trembled. "D-doctor, I just got word that the patients have broken out of the psycho ward and are heading this way."

"We do not use the word psycho in this institution," he replied calmly. "How many escaped?"

"All of them. W-we should evacuate while we can."

"I am in charge here, Amelia. I don't run. And neither do you. Now go back to your desk and let the guards handle this."

She stared at him, dumbstruck.

"Is there anything else, Amelia?"

"N-no, sir." The woman exited, closing the door behind her.

Dr. Savage opened the top right drawer, removed a .38 caliber revolver and a box of ammunition, and loaded six rounds into the chamber.

The sound of feet racing up the stairs accompanied by shouts calling for revenge echoed from the stairwell. Ten seconds later, he heard the door to the outer office slam open. A scuffle took place followed by Amelia screaming frantically in terror. The doctor grabbed the revolver and stood, waiting to engage the rioters.

The door to his office burst open and close to a dozen patients from the ward burst in led by Jacob. Jacob saw the pistol a moment before the doctor fired and ducked to the side. The first round hit the patient behind Jacob, blasting a gaping hole in his chest. He dropped to the floor, tripping those directly behind him. Dr. Savage emptied the last five rounds, taking down three more patients until the rest of the mob swarmed him and ripped the revolver from his hands. One patient aimed the barrel at the doctor's head and pulled the trigger. The hammer hit an empty chamber, making only a clicking sound.

"Stop," ordered Jacob. "The doctor's death cannot be so quick and easy."

A frenzy of insane excitement flowed through the mob.

Jacob got into the doctor's face. "What do you think of your special treatments now?"

"Obviously it did not work," Dr. Savage replied stoically. "Next time I'll increase the duration."

"There will be no next time." Spittle from Jacob's mouth covered the doctor's face.

Richard, one of the other patients, pushed Jacob aside. He clutched a rope in his hands. "String up the bastard."

Before Jacob could react, the mob grabbed Dr. Savage, dragged him from behind the desk, and stood him under the chandelier. Richard had looped one end into a noose. He placed it around the doctor's neck, then threw the other end over the chandelier. The other patients grabbed the loose end and pulled. When the rope tightened, rather than stringing up the doctor to suffocate, the chandelier tore from its mount and crashed to the floor, shattering into hundreds of pieces. The patients scattered. Dr. Savage stood there shaking his head.

"I see the treatments effected your ability to think properly."

The mob swarmed in.

"Stop." Jacob stepped up to the doctor and fixed his gaze on him. "This bastard deserves to suffer the same way we did. Bring him down to the treatment room."

The mob roared, lifted Dr. Savage off the floor, and carried him out of the office. The doctor did not struggle. He stoically observed the carnage that had befallen his asylum. Amelia being raped on her desk. The bodies of staff and security guards lying scattered along the corridors, one whose head had been bashed in so badly it was unrecognizable.

Eventually, they arrived at the treatment room. The mob threw the doctor onto the chair and strapped him down. Richard placed the electrodes on the doctor's head, laughing maniacally the whole time. Another patient, a serial killer whose name the doctor could not recall, switched on the ECT device, and set the power at two hundred and fifty volts. An electronic hum filled the room.

Jacob bent over and glared at Dr. Savage. "Now we'll have our revenge."

"You won't. I am in charge here. We may die, but we'll all be stuck here for eternity. Once we are, I plan to make your lives miserable."

An expression of fear flashed across Jacob's features but quickly faded. He turned to the device and pressed the button to engage treatment.

Two hundred and fifty volts flowed through Dr. Savage's body. His limbs convulsed. His body flopped against the chair. His eyes rolled up into his head. The doctor sensed his brain functions being burned away. He lost all his senses except that of hearing, which was overwhelmed by the sound of electronic crackling and the maniacal laughter of the patients watching him in his death throes.

Five seconds passed.

Ten seconds.

At the twelve second mark, the restraints on the doctor's right hand snapped. With his last bits of conscious thought, he reached out and clasped Jacob's hand. The voltage passed from one body to the other, electrocuting the patient as well.

"Tatyana."

Gayle's voice broke through the image, the word spoken softly yet laced with fear.

"Tatyana."

Tatyana snapped back to reality. As Tatyana looked up, she found herself staring into the spectral face of a tall and lanky man with dark hair and a thick mustache. He leaned over the front of the desk, his dark eyes fixed on her. She immediately recognized him from his photograph as Dr. Edmund Savage.

The long face broke into a sardonic smile.

"Hello, Tatyana."

CHAPTER FIFTEEN

"**Y**OU KNOW WHO I am?" Tatyana struggled not to stammer.

"How pretentious of you, young lady. If you can reach from your realm into ours and know who we are, then it only makes sense we can do the same." The doctor stood and clasped his hands behind his back. "You're Tatyana Reynolds, a self-taught paranormal investigator from New Hampshire. Unlike your colleagues here, you take your responsibilities seriously and concentrate on sending those spirits stuck in this world onward to the afterlife, whether they want to go willingly or not. You do this for the sake of the spirit world rather than personal popularity, which is admirable."

"You know a lot about me. You must also know I'm quite successful at what I do."

"No doubt. But this time, you will fail."

"Why is that?"

"Because I don't want to leave here." Dr. Savage glanced over at the paranormal team and smiled maliciously. "You can record all the activities you like. No one will ever see them."

"Why is that?" asked Daniel.

"Because none of you will be alive when Paul comes to pick you up in the morning."

An expression of horror washed over the team's faces.

Joel allowed his anger to get the better of him. "You can't keep us here. I won't allow—"

Dr. Savage flashed the producer with a glare so threatening it froze Joel in fear. "I can and I will."

Tatyana tried to regain control. "Why do you want us dead?"

"I don't, but it's a necessity. If you reveal my presence to the world, eventually someone will come to cleanse this facility and send us to the afterlife. I can't allow the spirits of the patients to be set free."

"What about the spirits of the staff and the patients who are innocent?" asked Gayle. "Why do they have to suffer?"

"Again, my dear woman. A necessity. I can't allow everything I've achieved here to be undone."

Tatyana forced a laugh. "What have you done? You mistreated your patients so badly they revolted and murdered you and your staff."

"On the contrary, I was too lenient with them. As inhumane as my methods of treatment seem to you, they successfully curbed the violent instincts of those in what you call the psycho ward. If I had increased the number and intensity of the treatments beforehand, the riot would never have occurred."

"Bullshit," said Daniel.

"I have more control over my patients now than I ever have." The doctor focused his attention back on Tatyana, fixing her gaze as he pointed to Nick. "Ask your spectral friend. He'll verify it."

Nick sighed. "It's true. Every spirit in this building is terrified of him. He has complete reign over them."

"What did he say?" asked Daniel.

"That Dr. Savage has complete control over every patient in this hospital and they're terrified of him."

"I don't buy that," said Daniel. "If you had control over the ghosts here, why would you let them kill us?"

"Let them?" Dr. Savage walked over and stared at Daniel. "I ordered them to."

Loud, crazed yells emanated from the stairwell.

Gayle stared at the EMF detector in her hand. "Jesus, the

levels have spiked into the red."

The spirit box came to life with a myriad of voices jumbled together in maniacal anger. Every few seconds, one voice spoke louder than the others, the words coming through clearly over the spirit box.

"Kill!"

"Murder!"

"Death to them all!"

"WH-WHAT THE HELL is that?" stammered Miles who watched over Hae-jin's shoulder.

Hae-jin stared at the monitor, too shocked to answer. She had been doing this job for years but had never witnessed anything like this before. The spectral image of fifteen people dressed as patients raced up the center stairwell toward Dr. Savage's office.

She picked up the two-way radio and pressed the talk button. "Daniel, can you hear me?"

Electronic static came over the speaker.

"Daniel, can you hear me?'

Still electronic static.

"Daniel, they're coming for you. The ghosts are on their way."

Still no answer.

Hae-jin grabbed a flashlight and headed for the stairwell. "Come on. We got to warn them."

"No way." Miles stepped back and shook his head.

Hae-jin paused long enough to come back, grab Miles by the collar, and drag him along with her.

TATYANA HEARD THE spirits rampaging through the stairwell and knew what would happen next. So did Nostradamus, who moved in front of his mistress. His ears lowered back on his head. His fangs bared. The dog snarled.

"Enough," Tatyana said to Dr. Savage. "You've made your point."

The doctor, who stood in front of Daniel, spun around to face her. "I'm not trying to make a point. I'm merely protecting what I've worked so hard for."

The approaching spirits grew louder.

"Please, call them off."

"You know I can't do that."

"Yes, you can."

"I won't." For one moment, the doctor's tone took on an almost sympathetic tone. "It's nothing personal."

The spirits surged through the door to Amelia's office and headed for the doctor's suite.

"Stop this now."

Dr. Savage turned away from Tatyana. As his spectral form dissolved into a mist, he pointed toward Daniel.

"This is the one."

"No!" Gayle rushed toward her husband.

A spirit moved between them, shoving the woman back against the wall as the rest swarmed around Daniel. Mac placed down the camera and went to help Daniel, as did Casey. Both men were held in place by spirits. Only Joel did nothing, moving back against the wall and closing his eyes in fear.

Tatyana took one step forward. "I command the entities in this room move on to the afterlife and leave us alone."

One of the spirits surrounding Daniel, a tall man with long scraggily hair and a deep scar across his face, broke away and charged her. Nostradamus lunged forward, startling the spirit long enough for Nick to move in to protect her.

"I address myself to the purest entities of the spiritual world," said Tatyana. "Help me drive away the entities in this room."

The spirits around Daniel surged forward, dragging him

across the floor and toward Tatyana. Clutching Nostradamus by the collar, she jumped to one side, pulling the dog out of the way. The spirits surged across the desk, dragging Daniel across the surface, and sent him crashing through the bay window. Daniel sailed into the air, surrounded by shards of shattered glass, and plummeted five stories to the pavement below. The sound of his body splattering against the cement wafted up through the broken window.

"Daniel." Gayle tried to go to the broken window to see her husband, only to be held in place by the spirit in front of her. She dropped to her knees and broke down, sobbing uncontrollably and repeatedly calling his name.

Tatyana rushed over to the window and leaned out, hoping for a miracle that Daniel was alive. The arms and legs twisted at perverse angles and the puddle of blood rapidly forming around his corpse confirmed her worst fears.

HAE-JIN REACHED THE fifth-floor landing of the stairwell and pushed open the outer door to the doctor's suite. Miles followed twenty feet behind her.

"Are you guys all right? A pack of ghosts are head—"

Four entities broke away from those by the window and flowed into the outer office. The smallest of them, a spirit with a demented laugh, grasped Hae-jin by the shoulders and slammed her against the wall, knocking the wind out of her.

Miles stopped in the outer doorway, shaken by what happened to his friend, staring at her in disbelief, oblivious to the danger in front of him. The other three spirits picked up Miles, dragged him onto the landing, and tossed him into the stairwell. His body landed on the bottom three steps, bounced off them with a loud cracking of bones, hit the western wall, and dropped onto the landing. Miles' body came to rest with his head at a ninety-degree angle.

THE SPIRIT HOLDING back Gayle yanked the woman to her feet. She screamed and struggled back, unable to break the spectral hold. It dragged Gayle toward the window to meet the same fate as her husband.

"Somebody, help me."

Joel stayed against the wall, too frightened to respond. He turned and averted his eyes.

Casey broke away from the spirit holding him back and rushed to help Gayle. Before he could reach her, three spirits tackled him to the ground. Two pinned each arm while the third clutched Casey by the hair and lifted his head, pointing to Gayle.

"Watch."

Mac tried pushing aside the spirit in front of him, a gargantuan of an entity standing over six feet tall and with biceps as large as Mac's legs. He made it only a few inches before the spirit clutched its hand around his neck, its fingers wrapped around the back of Mac's neck and its thumb pressing against his Adams' apple. It pushed Mac against the wall and lifted him a foot in the air. The hand closed around his throat, cutting off the supply of air.

Jacob limped his way toward Tatyana, a sadistic grin piercing his lips. Nostradamus lunged forward to stop the attacker, passing through the image. The dog skidded along the floor, reversed direction, and charged again. When Nostradamus got to within three feet, Jacob spun around and back handed the dog, sending him crashing into the doctor's desk.

Nick ran up alongside Tatyana and pushed her toward the exit. "Get out of here while you can."

"I'm not leaving the others behind."

"You heard the bitch." Jacob grabbed Nick by the back of the collar and threw him across the room. "She ain't leaving."

"I address myself to the purest entities of the spiritual world," said Tatyana. "Help me drive away the en—"

Jacob grabbed Tatyana by the hair, forced the woman to

her knees, and pulled her head back. He ran his tongue across his lips.

Tatyana glanced around the office. Daniel was dead and Gayle was about to join him. One spirit strangled Mac. The entities had taken Nick, Nostradamus, and Casey out of the fight and would eliminate them soon. Only Joel had been left untouched, and only because he was a miserable coward who posed no threat. Tatyana realized she had miscalculated big time, and it would cost all of them their lives. She was not dealing with spirits who could be reasoned with, or whose emotions could be invoked, but rather with psychopaths who thrived on violence led by a narcissistic control freak determined to use the afterlife to prove his barbaric theories. She only hoped her death would be less horrific than the others.

Tatyana closed her eyes and waited for death.

"Enough." Dr. Savage's voice echoed through his office.

Tatyana opened her eyes. The spirits had paused their assault, though she could still sense a lust for violence and revenge. For a moment, she thought the entities might ignore the command.

Apparently, so did the doctor.

"I told you to stand down."

The spirits cowered a bit, but still did not stop fully.

"You do not want me ask a third time."

Tatyana felt her hair being released as the entities withdrew.

Mac fell to the floor, holding his throat and gasping for breath.

Gayle was released a yard from the shattered bay window, falling to her hands and knees, sobbing from fear and heartache. Tatyana climbed to her feet and ran over to help, crouching beside Gayle and placing a hand on her shoulders.

"Are you okay?"

"Of course, I'm not okay." Gayle shook herself loose. "My husband is dead."

Gayle struggled to stand and move toward the window. Tatyana held her back. "You don't want to see him."

"Get away from me." Gayle shoved away Tatyana.

Tatyana hugged the distraught woman, this time refusing to let go. Gayle struggled for several seconds before collapsing into Tatyana's arms, sobbing uncontrollably. Tatyana wrapped her arms tight around Gayle, rocking her back and forth.

Nick and Nostradamus joined them a few seconds later, the latter licking his mistress' face. Tatyana reached over with her free hand and scratched his chest.

"Are you okay?" asked Nick.

"I will be one we get out of here."

Casey joined them. "What happened? Why did the doctor let us go?"

Tatyana looked up at him. "I think the doctor has something worse planned for us."

"That's what I was afraid you were going to say."

Joel stepped up. "What could be worse than what he's already put us through?"

Casey swung around and punched Joel in the jaw, almost knocking him unconscious. The producer staggered back, tripping over his feet and crashing to the floor. Casey went after him again. Joel closed his eyes and flinched.

Mac interceded, standing in front of Casey and holding him back. "Let it go."

"The little shit did nothing to help us."

"I was scared," whined Joel.

"We were all scared," said Tatyana. "We have to figure a way out of this situation or none of us are going to make it to morning. Joel, either step up to the plate and help or stay out of our way."

Joel climbed to his feet, massaged his bruised jaw, and distanced himself from the others.

Hae-jin staggered into the office. "Is everything okay in here?"

Tatyana shook her head.

Hae-jin saw the shattered bay window. "Who?"

"Daniel."

Hae-jin's hand covered her mouth. "Gayle, I'm so sorry."

"Why are you up here?" Casey asked out of curiosity.

"I saw the spirits heading this way. Your radios didn't work, so we came up here to warn you. We were too late."

Tatyana picked up on the word we. "Where's Miles?"

"They ambushed us in the outer office. Miles is dead."

Casey mumbled the F-word under his breath.

Tatyana helped Gayle to her feet. "Gather the equipment and let's get out of here."

"Do we need it?" asked Gayle. "We're done with the investigation."

"The EMF detectors will warn us if the spirits are coming after us."

CHAPTER SIXTEEN

T HEY PLACED MILES' body on the floor by Robert. Since Dr. Savage still wouldn't allow them outside, Daniel's corpse remained out front.

As Tatyana, Nick, Gayle, and Casey sat in the center of the lobby trying to determine their next move, Hae-jin reviewed all the videos to see if they had picked up everything that had taken place upstairs. Joel sat by himself near the front door.

Casey glanced over at Hae-jin. "Why bother with that stuff? No one cares about the investigation anymore."

"I want to make sure there's a record of what happened in case we don't make it."

"Morbid."

"Who knows." She forced a smile. "Maybe someday they'll make a found-footage movie about us."

Tatyana rolled her eyes. "God, I hope not."

"Back to the matter at hand," said Nick. "How do we stop the doctor?"

"I was hoping you could answer that." Tatyana smiled.

"This one has me stumped. Dr. Savage has complete control over the entities here. Right now, he's toying with you. The only reason you all didn't die upstairs was because he stopped them. It's only a few hours to sunrise. The next attack will be the last."

"Talking to your friend Nick?" asked Gayle.

"Yes." Tatyana related what he had told her.

Casey sighed. "What if we stay here and hope for the best?"

Tatyana shook her head. "The entities can go anywhere in

this building. If we stay put, the doctor will just send them to get us."

Joel stood and joined the others. "What about using the other entities against them?"

"What entities?" asked Gayle.

"The ones that are not part of the psycho club, like that girl who talked to Tatyana in the treatment room, and the ghosts of those who were victims of the riot. We could organize a strike."

The others stared at Joel as if he had snakes sprouting from his head.

"Everyone knows who the actors and directors are, but no one cares about the production staff. Yet, if they get pissed off and go on strike, the movie doesn't get made."

"I hate to say it," said Casey. "It makes sense."

"That's how we got rid of Kathleen at Eden Hollow," added Nick.

"But will they help us?" asked Hae-jin. "They're terrified of him."

"They have been helping us. Hopefully, they'll realize this is their only chance to be free of him."

Hae-jin did not seem convinced. "What if they refuse to help, or are unable to stop him?"

Joel shrugged. "It's worth a try. We're dead in either case. At least this way we go out fighting."

"Then let's do it," said Casey.

"One question," said Joel. "Where do we find these ghosts."

Tatyana knew the answer but did not like it. "We'll have to return to the treatment room where they first contacted us."

CHAPTER SEVENTEEN

T HE SURVIVING MEMBERS of the paranormal investigation team left the lobby and made their way into the center stairwell, their numbers having dwindled from the original ten down to six. The truth nobody wanted to face was there may be even fewer of them alive by morning.

Tatyana and Nostradamus led the way with Gayle close behind and to her left, holding an EMF detector. Casey followed with a spirit box. Mac kept the camera with him, filming the entire time. Tatyana had asked him to do so not for the sake of the documentary, which would never be made, but to document what went down in the next few minutes in case none of them survived to tell their story. Joel brought up the rear along with Hae-jin, who refused to stay alone, each carrying a spare EMF detector and spirit box, respectively. Each kept their head-mounted flashlights on, more concerned to see what transpired around them than picking up any spiritual presence.

The entities in Bethlehem Asylum had no qualms about showing themselves when they wanted to.

They exited onto the basement corridor and paused. Gayle moved up alongside Tatyana, her eyes focused on the detector.

"I'm picking up nothing. Are you getting anything?"

"Not even a hum." Tatyana glanced down at Nostradamus. The dog looked up, smiled, and wagged his tail. She turned to the others. "You're all familiar with the plan?"

"We should be." Joel had a heavy snark in his tone. "We went over it enough times."

"Because we're not going to get a second chance at this. Next time, I don't think the doctor is going to call off the patients."

Hae-jin grew nervous. "I hope none of them overheard what we're planning."

"Doubtful. Either me, Nostradamus, or the EMF detector would have picked up a spiritual presence if one had been listening in."

"And if you're wrong?" asked Joel.

Tatyana grinned. "Then this won't take long. Come on."

The group slowly made their way down the corridor.

In the back, Joel mumbled, "That's not funny."

The door to the treatment room sat open. Gayle took Tatyana by the arm and stopped her.

"Tanner's still in there."

"Should we take him out?" asked Casey.

"We don't have time." Tatyana thought for a moment. "Do we have anything we can cover him with?"

"Use this." Hae-jin slid off her fishing vest and handed it to Tatyana.

"Wait here."

Tatyana entered the room. Tanner's corpse lay on the reclining chair. Portions of his skin hung loose where his body swelled during the electrocution. The skin around his temples where the electrodes were attached showed signs of third-degree burns, the surrounding flesh charred black. Tanner's left eye sat bulging in its socket. Dried blood from his nose ran down his face. The front and rear of his pants were stained from where he had relieved himself. The stench of urine, feces, and burnt flesh hung in the air. Tatyana fought back tears at both the agony and indignity of Tanner's demise.

She placed the vest over his face. "All clear."

The others entered and formed a circle around the chair. Mac placed the camera in one corner facing the center of the room.

Gayle took a deep breath. "What now?"

Tatyana stepped over to the chair. Her voice sounded more like a whisper than a summoning.

"I'm addressing myself to the spirit who reached out to me earlier, the young lady whose baby died at birth."

An eerie silence.

"I want to talk to the spirit whose baby died at birth."

Nothing.

"I'm not here to harm you. Please respond."

A few seconds passed. Gayle became excited. "I have a spike in the reading."

"How much?"

"Halfway through the yellow zone."

Tatyana spoke a little louder. "We want to help you."

The spirit box crackled, startling Casey.

"We didn't hear you. Please say it again."

More silence.

"It must have left," said Joel. "Maybe we should get out of here, too."

Tatyana ignored him. "Please repeat yourself."

The spirit box crackled. A female voice came over the speaker. "Go away."

"We can't. We're stuck here the same as you are. We can help each other escape."

"Oh, shit." Joel pointed to the corner of the room.

The spectral image of the young woman emerged from the shadows. Fear distorted her features.

"Please, go away. You'll make the doctor angry, and he'll release the bad spirits on us."

"He will whether we stay here or go back to the lobby. The only way we can stop him and save ourselves, including you and those spirits trapped here, is if you help us fight them."

"No." The spirit shook her head furiously.

"Then we're all doomed here for eternity."

"Please leave before…." The entity paused. "It's too late."

"The detector is all the way in the red." Gayle glanced up, terror in her eyes.

Tatyana did not need to be warned. She felt the increasing presence of Dr. Savage and his gang of psychos.

✕   ✕   ✕

NICK DID NOT join Tatyana and the others. What they were doing was merely a distraction. Instead, he roamed the second-floor corridor, mentally calling out to the tortured spirits who existed in this facility who had been scared into submission.

"I need to talk to the spirits who are trapped here and want to leave."

He felt their presence, but also their unwillingness to talk to him.

"Please, speak to me. I'm one of you."

"You don't belong here," a female voice sounded in his head.

"I know."

"Then what are you doing here?"

"I'm with Tatyana, the spiritualist who's trying to help you."

"She can't help us. She and her human friends will wind up joining us in this hellhole. Several of them already have."

Nick chose his words carefully. "We can help you, all of you, but you have to be willing to help us."

"We can't."

Nick delved into the woman's soul, recognizing her as the young woman who had given birth to the stillborn child.

"What's your name?"

"Sandra."

"Sandra, how many of you are there? I mean, how many are here besides Dr. Savage and the psycho ward patients?"

"We find that term offensive." Her voice softened. "There are thirty-nine of us trapped here."

"How did you die?"

"I was hanged by the patients during the riot," replied a male staff member.

"I was shot by one of the guards who mistook me for one of the rioters."

"Three of the patients brutally raped and butchered me," responded Amelia, the doctor's secretary.

A litany of stories followed, each one swarming through Nick's thoughts. Some were staff members and nurses who had never mistreated patients yet were slaughtered by the rioters for merely being there at the time of the riot. A few who were mistakenly shot by guards so panicked they could not tell the dangerous ward patients from those merely there for other reasons. Guards who had been murdered for attempting to stop the violence. Innocent patients who died as part of the carnage. They had all lost their lives that nightmarish evening. And when Dr. Savage, in his final moments of life, condemned the patients from the dangerous patient ward to eternal damnation in the hospital, he inadvertently condemned all of them. Since then, these entities had lived in terror of the chaos that could be caused by the doctor and his gang, remaining dormant in the shadows rather than endure further suffering.

"I can empathize with what you went through."

Thirty-nine souls protested at once. Sandra quieted them down.

"You have no idea what we endured here."

"You're right, I can't comprehend the extent of your suffering. But I empathize. I was murdered by my wife and was terrified by her spirit for as long as you. Since then, I've connected with those in the afterlife, some of whom have gone through trauma as bad as yours. And in every instance, when those spirits have been willing to work with us, they've been able to peacefully move on."

Sandra shook her head. "It won't work here."

"It will if you have the courage to stand up to Dr. Savage

and his bunch."

"We... we can't."

A sense of evil arose within the corridor. Nick felt it as the other gathered spirits began to panic.

Sandra flashed him a frightened look. "They're on the move."

"Savage and his group?"

"Yes."

"Are they coming after you?"

"No. Your friends."

"This is your last chance. Help them and we can set your souls free."

"Can you guarantee that?"

Nick refused to lie. "No."

"Then why should we risk the doctor's wrath?"

"If you don't, you'll be stuck here forever. If you try, at least you have a fighting chance."

A wave of conflicting opinions from the other entities bombarded Sandra. She merely stared at Nick, fear and uncertainty in her expression.

CHAPTER EIGHTEEN

TATYANA SWALLOWED HARD. The next few minutes were literally a matter of life and death.

"Is everyone ready?"

The others formed a circle around her. Nostradamus moved beside his mistress and leaned into her leg. They chanted in unison.

"Purest entities of the spectral world, grant me the strength to banish the vile spirits that haunt this realm and cause so much suffering to the innocent. Help me to thrust into Hell the malevolent entity that dwells in this institution, that commands the spirits of those who it tortured to do its bidding, and that thrives off the misery and suffering of those who are trapped here who are good and righteous."

The call only served to rile up the entities even more.

"Purest entities of the spectral world, grant me the strength to banish the vile spirits that haunt this realm and cause so much suffering to the innocent. Help me to thrust into Hell the malevolent entity that dwells in this institution, that commands the spirits of those who it tortured to do its bidding, and that thrives off the misery and suffering of those who are trapped here who are good and righteous."

The spirit box erupted. Static flowed from the speakers with specific words occasionally breaking through the background noise.

"Fools."

"Get them!"

"Kill!"

"It's not working," warned Gayle.

Joel sneered. "No shit."

"Don't stop." Tatyana started to recite the chant, this time by herself. "We must present a united front."

The others joined in.

"Purest entities of the spectral world, grant me the strength to banish the vile spirits that haunt this realm and cause so much suffering to the innocent. Help me to thrust into Hell the malevolent–"

Dr. Savage materialized in front of Tatyana. "Your determination is becoming annoying. I'd think by now you'd realize you can't win against me."

"Good always triumphs over evil."

The doctor laughed, the gesture more gruesome in his spirit form. "You sound like all those who opposed my methods."

"It seems they were right."

"On the contrary. My methods were effective, I just wasn't tough enough. If I had been a little tougher, they would have been cured. In a way, it worked out well for me. They now do my bidding because they respect me."

"They do your bidding because they fear you."

Dr. Savage leaned in closer and whispered, "As they should."

A cold chill raced down Tatyana's spine.

"Purest entities of the spectral world, grant me the strength to banish the vile–"

Dr. Savage frowned and walked away from Tatyana. "Jacob."

The spirits of the fifteen patients from the dangerous patient ward materialized throughout the room.

"Yes, doctor?"

"Finish the job. Leave no one alive."

Sadistic glee filled the room.

Three of the patients attacked Gayle, fondling the terrified woman before dragging her to the floor.

One went after Hae-jin. He shoved her against the wall and wrapped his hands around her neck, his thumbs covering her Adam's apple, and tightened his grip, closing off her airways.

Two entities taunted Joel, standing in front of the producer, slapping and teasing him. Joel fell to his knees and cried.

One each held Casey, Mac, and Nostradamus. The dog growled and bit at the entity holding him, his efforts having no effect.

"What are you doing?" asked Casey.

"Letting you wait your turn." The spirit motioned toward the treatment chair.

Jacob held Tatyana in place while the five remaining patients unstrapped Tanner's body, removed it from the chair, and dropped it to the floor. It made a sickening thud and flopped to one side. They then took Tatyana from Jacob and dragged her to the chair. She fought, her efforts succeeding only in making the spirits laugh harder. The patients placed her in the chair and held her down as Jacob secured the straps around her limbs and chest.

Dr. Savage picked up the electrodes from the small metal table and tried to place them on Tatyana's temples. She thrashed her head around to prevent him from putting them on. Jacob grabbed Tatyana's cheeks, squeezing them tight and holding her head in place. The doctor slid on the electrodes and secured them with a head strap. Jacob moved over to the device and flipped the on switch. An electronic hum filled the room.

Dr. Savage leaned over, his face hovering over Tatyana's. "I admire your determination. I'm sorry it has to end this way."

Tatyana struggled not to let her fear show. "You don't have to do this."

"Unfortunately, I do. My secret must be kept if I'm to reign over this institution."

The doctor reached behind him for the ECT treatment button.

A hand already rested on top of it.

Dr. Savage spun around to face Sandra. She glared at him. Fear showed in her eyes, but so did a determination to end this nightmare.

"It's over, doctor."

"Not until I say it is."

"It's time this ended. Let them go."

The doctor chuckled. "Do you really think one young woman is going to stop me?"

"Of course not." Sandra allowed the slightest hint of a smile to pierce her lips. "But I'm not alone."

The remaining entities materialized throughout the treatment room, catching Dr. Savage and his underlings off guard.

Six female entities, both nurses and patients, yanked the three attackers off Gayle. Not anticipating the arrival of these until-now-dormant entities and surprised by their aggression, the psychos backed down. Two stepped away, lifting their hands to show they had stopped. The third dropped to his knees out of fear. Seventy years of pent-up anger boiled over. Rather than let the attackers go, the six female entities mercilessly beat them. As the assault grew increasingly violent, the psychos became more subdued.

Three security guards and a female patient surrounded Hae-jin's assailant. The guards pulled away the attacker, threw him to the ground, and subdued him. Hae-jin slid to the floor, gasping for air. The female patient crouched beside her, offering comfort until she was certain the human would survive.

The patient holding Casey released him and rushed to help the doctor. The spirit of the mother of the stillborn baby materialized in front of him. The expression of anger on her face and the hatred glaring in her eyes frightened the entity. She wailed at him. The entity morphed into a mist and dissipated. Casey ignored the confrontation, instead going to Gayle's assistance.

The spirits holding Mac and Nostradamus released their grips. The dog spun around and barked at its captor, scaring the entity enough that it backed away. Nostradamus ran over to Nick, who appeared by the chair and loosened Tatyana's restraints. Mac ran over to check on Hae-jin.

Dr. Savage turned to initiate the ECT treatment. Sandra still held her hand over the button.

"Step away," the doctor growled.

"You're no longer in charge here."

Two male patients each grabbed Dr. Savage by an arm. He attempted to break free, but they held him in place. The doctor stopped struggling and met Sandra's gaze.

"Release me or I'll make your lives a living hell."

"You already have. Now it's our turn."

Nick and the others finished unstrapping Tatyana and helped her out of the chair. They moved away several feet and stopped. Nostradamus placed himself between Dr. Savage and his mistress.

Sandra nodded. The two guards hoisted the doctor onto the chair. James, Nyby, and Amelia came over and secured the restraints around his ankles, wrists, and chest. Margaret slid the electrodes over his temple and strapped them down.

"What do you think you're doing?" asked the doctor with contempt in his voice. "This will have no effect on me."

"It will. And once you're gone, we're free to move on to the afterlife."

Fury raged inside Dr. Savage. "You're all going to regret this."

"Doctor, as you're so fond of saying...." Sandra placed her hand on the button. "Enough."

She pressed the button.

Two hundred and fifty volts of electricity flowed through the doctor. He closed his eyes and grimaced, though he felt no pain. The current broke down his spiritual form. Pieces of his essence separated and floated upward in tufts of mist, dissipating in the air. The breakdown increased with each passing second until the doctor's face relaxed and his body expanded into a fog-like cloud. The restraints went slack. The electrodes clattered to the floor.

Dr. Savage had gone to whatever afterlife awaited him.

Around them, the other entities fell apart and wafted skyward. The faces of those from the dangerous patient ward showed fear, most knowing what fate awaited them. The guards, staff members, and other patients seemed serene and happy. Several glanced toward the paranormal investigation team, nodding in gratitude. A few stretched their arms toward the heavens, welcoming their journey.

Sandra stepped over to Nick. She placed a hand on his chin, leaned in close, and kissed him on the right cheek.

"Thank you."

"We should be thanking you."

Sandra smiled in embarrassment, stepped back a few feet, and waved. Three seconds later, her form had vanished.

The background hum of the spirits died off. Tatyana felt a much-needed serenity fill the corridors. Bethlehem Asylum was devoid of any spectral entities.

Mac removed the EMF detector he had slid into his pocket. "I'm picking up no signal."

"Does that mean they're gone?" asked Gayle.

"I think so."

"They're gone," confirmed Nick. "I can't feel any spectral presence."

Tatyana passed the news to the others. She and Nostradamus went over to check on Gayle who still sat on the floor recovering from the shock of her attack.

"Are you hurt?'

Gayle shook her head. "Just badly shaken and a little bruised."

Tatyana glanced up, noticing Joel still cowering against the wall. The look of disdain she flashed him made the producer bow his head in shame. Instead, she turned her attention to Hae-jin.

"How are you?"

"I'm okay," coughed Hae-jin. "I never realized ghosts could physically harm you that way."

"More often than you think."

Casey and Tatyana helped Gayle to her feet.

"Can you stand?"

"Yes, thanks. What happened?"

Casey answered. "Nick's plan to rally the other spirits against the doctor must have worked."

"Of course, it did," joked Nick, even though only Tatyana could hear him. "It was my plan."

Tatyana rolled her eyes.

Gayle pointed to the chair. "I mean, what happened to Dr. Savage? I didn't think spirits could be electrocuted."

"As far as I know, they can't." Tatyana stepped over to the chair and ran her hand across it. "I don't think it was the electrocution so much as uprising of the spirits who have been dominated over. When Sandra pressed the button, it signified they had had enough. When the doctor's control over this place was removed so was his spectral entity. The remaining spirits were able to move on."

"I wonder where they are now?" asked Hae-jin.

"Who friggin' cares," mumbled Joel.

Tatyana shrugged. "I'd like to think they're getting the afterlife they deserved based on how they lived in this realm."

Gayle closed her eyes. "Amen."

Mac checked his watch. "We better get downstairs and pack things up. Paul will be here in an hour."

CHAPTER NINETEEN

W ITH THE INSTITUTION cleansed of spirits, the team was able to open the main entrance and retrieve Daniel's body. They placed it on the floor beside those of Robert, Tanner, and Miles. Gayle stayed with her husband, holding his hand and sobbing.

Mac and Casey made a quick round of the locations inside the facility they had conducted investigations in to make certain none of their equipment had been left behind. As they made their rounds, Hae-jin packed up the camera and monitors. She checked the files first, amazed to find that all the footage taken by the twin cameras was not only intact, including the final confrontation with Dr. Savage in the treatment room, but the film quality remained excellent. She backed up the files and saved them, then broke everything down. Hae-jin ordered Joel to take the containers outside and pile them up so they could be loaded in Paul's van. Joel said nothing and did as he was told.

When the last of the equipment had been moved to the driveway, most of the team stayed outside to avoid spending any more time than necessary inside the asylum. Only Gayle and Tatyana remained behind, with Nostradamus hovering around his mistress. Tatyana gave her friend a few minutes to mourn, then crossed the room and stood behind her.

"It's time to go."

"No," Gayle whispered beneath a sob. "I can't leave him."

"It's only temporary."

Gayle shook her head.

Tatyana gently placed a hand on her shoulder. "He'll be

fine. You'll be together by the end of the day."

Gayle sighed. She leaned forward, patted Daniel's chest, and kissed his forehead through the blanket. Standing, she wiped the tears from her eyes, but kept her gaze focused on the covered body. Taking her by the hand, Tatyana gently led Gayle to the entrance.

"I'll join you in a minute."

Gayle nodded. As she exited, Nostradamus followed, staying close to the woman for comfort.

Nick materialized beside her. "Do you think she'll be okay?"

"Maybe, but she'll never be the same again. You don't get over losing a loved one so easily."

"Unless they murdered you," teased Nick.

Tatyana chuckled despite the dark humor. "Did you do a sweep of the asylum?"

"Yeah. There's no residual presence anywhere. I even checked the ward, treatment room, and Dr. Savage's office."

"Good. Their souls are finally at peace."

"Do you plan on telling their story?"

"If I told the story of every spirit I sent on, I would never get anything done."

"This is different," said Nick. "A lot of what went on in this place has been kept hidden from the public for over seventy years. Don't you think people should know the truth and how the patients suffered?"

"I can't write a book about this. I'd be profiting off other's misery."

"What about them?" Nick pointed outside to the investigation team. "You could tell the story as part of their program. It would explain what happened during the attacks."

"I seriously doubt the series will ever air now that Daniel and so many members of his team are gone. Gayle wouldn't approve. No, this is one of those stories that will remain undocumented. Only we'll know the good we did."

Paul pulled his van up to the exterior gate. He climbed out of his vehicle, unlocked the gate, opened it, then got back in and headed up the driveway.

"I'll let you go. You'll be busy for a while." As Nick dissolved into a mist, he added, "Good luck."

Once Nick had disappeared, Tatyana said, "Thanks. I'll need it."

Tatyana exited the building and descended the stairs, reaching the driveway as Paul stepped out of his van.

"Morning. I told you I'd be here at six to pick you up. Where's the rest of your group?"

All eyes fell on Tatyana. She took a deep breath.

"You're not going to believe what I'm about to tell you."

CHAPTER TWENTY

Eight Months Later

TATYANA WORKED AT her desk, finishing her dissertation. Nick sat on the sofa, watching television, the volume turned down so it did not bother her. Nostradamus lay on the sofa, curled up and asleep beside Nick.

As much as Tatyana tried to forget what had happened that night at Bethlehem Asylum, the memories were burned in her mind. As bad as the events of that evening were the following three days. At first, the local and State Police refused to believe that spirits had killed Daniel, Robert, Tanner, and Miles. They assumed someone else had taken their lives and the survivors were covering it up. Not that she blamed them. Before she had become a paranormal investigator and experienced such encounters herself, she would not have believed it. Even after the authorities watched the footage of the deaths, they refused to be convinced, suspicious that Tatyana and the others had faked the film to cover their actions. Only after two media experts were brought in and testified the footage was authentic did the police let everyone go.

Once the investigation team parted ways at the airport, Tatyana heard little from them. Joel barely spoke a dozen words to her during the three days of the police investigation and did not even bother to see her off. She assumed the coward was too embarrassed to show his face. The rest of Daniel's team came to say goodbye. Casey never contacted Tatyana or returned her messages. She and Hae-jin chatted once or twice, but only briefly. Tatyana and Gayle talked for several months. However, the loss of Daniel ate away at Gayle, and her conversations with Tatyana became fewer and more morose until they ended all together. Not that she could blame any of them. If this had been her first paranormal experience, Tatyana would have committed herself to an institution, albeit one better run than Bethlehem.

In fact, the experience had been so disturbing for Tatyana she had not undertaken any investigations since Bethlehem Asylum, concentrating instead on finishing her doctorate, partially because she needed to complete it and partially as an excuse to not delve into the realm of the paranormal. Of course, she missed it. Being able to communicate with the afterlife was a gift, and she considered helping those spirits stuck in limbo a calling she could not avoid. However, after losing four friends during the last investigation, she was afraid to get involved again.

"You'll do another one when you're up to it," said Nick from the sofa.

"Do another what?"

"An investigation. It's in your blood."

"Are you reading my mind?" asked Tatyana with an accusatory tone.

"I don't have to. I know you too well. You feel this way after every difficult investigation. And each time you agree to take on cases that are worse than the previous one." Nick leaned his head back so he could see her. "It's imbedded in your nature."

Though Tatyana would not admit it, Nick was right. She knew that eventually she would return to conducting paranormal investigations.

She went back to work, Nick resumed watching television, and Nostradamus continued napping.

A few minutes later, Nick blurted out, "That bastard."

"What are you talking about?"

"Look at this." Nick turned up the television volume.

Joel stood in a studio decorated to look like a Tarot reading room. He did a slow walk through the set as he spoke.

"Welcome to the premiere episode of *Paranormal Explained.* I'm Joel Carbone. Tonight, we'll be delving into the most disturbing haunting since Amityville in 1975. I led a paranormal investigation of Bethlehem Asylum near Craig, Colorado, an institution with a dark past that rivals some of the most bizarre medical facilities in history. We conducted an overnight stay at the asylum."

As Joel talked, video clips taken of each participant the night of the incident flashed across the screen for three seconds with their name underneath. Tatyana was listed last.

"Each of us went in not knowing the nightmares we would face. Some of those who entered Bethlehem Asylum that night did not live long enough to see the dawn. This show is dedicated to them.

"Everything that was recorded during the investigation, including the deaths of my friends, has been included in this broadcast. Viewer discretion is advised. Having said that, get ready to watch our paranormal investigation of Bethlehem Asylum."

The show cut into a five-minute segment, narrated by Joel, of the history of the institution and the riot that occurred in March 1951. Following the introduction, it went into the meeting of the team, their arrival at the asylum, and the horrifying events that took place. The footage had been edited to exclude all of Joel's cowardly moments and additional interview spots were added to make him appear as the leader and hero of the team. To his credit, Joel included the full footage of all the deaths and the final confrontation between Dr. Savage and the abused patients, though Tatyana knew that was done for the purpose of ratings and not to pay homage to those who lost their lives. When the show finished, Joel appeared back in the studio with a few wrap-up remarks before thanking the audience for joining them. The program ended with photos of those who had died that night accompanied by the years of their births and deaths, then the end credits rolled.

Nick shut off the television. "I can't believe the son of a bitch aired that show after what happened."

"I can."

"He made himself look like the hero of that night."

Tatyana shrugged. "He's the producer. He can do anything he wants."

A ping announced she had received an email. It was from Gayle.

Sorry. I don't know if you watched the show. I only just saw it myself. Joel sent the rest of us an email last night saying that if we publicly voiced any objections to it, the studio would come after us with every legal means at their disposal. I wished it hadn't turned out this way. Sorry again.

Tatyana deleted the email.

Nick huffed from the sofa. "I should go haunt that asshole. What do you think?"

For a moment, Tatyana considered letting him do it. Joel deserved whatever happened to him. But she thought better about it. It wasn't like he would learn anything from it.

"Leave Joel alone. He's not—"

Tatyana's cellphone rang. She picked it up from the desk. The phone number was from an unknown caller with a 202-area code. She accepted it.

"Hello?"

"Is this Tatyana Reynolds?" The man on the other end spoke excellent English though with a heavy East European accent.

"Who's calling?"

"I'm with the Polish Embassy in Washington D.C. Ambassador Wojciechowski is on the other line. He wants to talk to you."

"About what?"

"About a situation we have here in our country."

PREVIEW OF
THE DEADLIEST BREED OF ASSASSINS

Southern Iraq
31 March, 3:49 AM Arab Standard Time (AST)

H E SLOWLY EMERGED from his unconscious state. As the void faded, it gave way to the sensation of motion, a swaying back and forth as if floating. He forced his eyes open. It took several seconds for his vision to adapt to the limited light provided by the full moon. He glanced around, only vaguely aware that he hovered thirty feet above the sun-bleached sands of a desert. He was cognizant of being flown yet did not comprehend that the vehicle which transported him was a makeshift mini-helicopter comprised of eighteen four-blade propellers linked together in a circular array with an eighteen-foot wingspan. He sat in an open cockpit mounted underneath the engine array.

Three miles ahead of him, the moon reflected off the shimmering surface of a river. Beyond that, along the river's southern bank, the lights of a small city glared, burning away the natural luminescence of the moon. As with the mini-helicopter that carried him, the river and city held no significance, although on a subconscious level he could not divert his attention from them.

The man delved into his own mind for the answers to questions he had not consciously formulated. Who was he? What was going on? Why was he here? The situation possessed a familiarity about it. A recollection buried deep in the recesses of his psyche told him he had done something like this before. He followed that memory, hoping to solve the mystery of his missing life.

Vague images flashed through his thoughts. A beautiful woman with olive skin and a loving smile. A child no more than eight years old stared at him with adoring eyes. Although on some level he knew these people were important to him, the man did not recognize them or the emotional spark they generated. His recalled disjointed voices, which aroused feelings within him, much different and more intense than those associated with the woman and child. A distant part of his mind warned him that the voices were associated with pain and fear, emotions he could not define but viscerally recognized as negative. The voices without faces spoke in a language he did not understand. However, they repeated one word with enough frequency that it stuck—Oscar.

The revelation came to him. His name must be Oscar.

A burst of adrenalin cleared his mind, and piece by piece Oscar comprehended the environment around him. Ahead of him flowed the Shatt al-Arab River and, beyond that, the city of Basrah. His gaze followed the riverbank to the south until he focused on the palace that had once belonged to Saddam Hussein. After the war, the government converted it into an antiquities museum. With the spread of Iranian-backed Islamic fundamentalism throughout southern Iraq, the grounds had been taken over by *jihadists* and the palace converted into the headquarters for *Shaykh* al-Sayyid Muhammad al-Sistani, the local commander of the Islamic State of Iraq and Syria.

And Oscar's target for assassination.

As the mini-helicopter approached to within a thousand yards of the Shatt al-Arab, it descended until it skimmed the desert, blending into the shadows of the night. Its forward movement stopped short of the river. It hovered for a moment, and then moved sideways along the northern bank searching for a location to covertly insert him. Out of instinct, Oscar also searched for an infiltration point. At first, it seemed he would not find one. Guards patrolled the length of the compound, most concentrating around the entrance gate to the northwest and the main palace to the southeast, while two-man teams guarded each of the separate buildings. Only in the center, where the perimeter road stretched across a strip of land sandwiched between the riverbank and a man-made lake, was there a large enough gap for him to land undetected.

The mini-helicopter surged forward, dashing across the river at an altitude of only a few feet. It climbed at the last moment, clearing the bank and road, before stopping by the edge of the man-made lake. In one instinctive, fluid motion Oscar unstrapped himself, jumped out of his seat, removed the hunting knife from the sheath attached to his right leg, and fell prone onto the dirt. The drone turned one hundred and eighty degrees and accelerated back across the Shatt al-Arab, disappearing into the night. Oscar remained on the ground, giving his senses enough time to adjust to his new surroundings.

Unzipping the right leg pocket of his olive drab Nomex flightsuit, Oscar removed a pair of night vision binoculars, switched them on, and scanned the compound. A few hundred yards to the right sat a large ornate building bordering the perimeter road. Another few hundred yards beyond that was the man-made island that held the compound's administrative and security buildings. The palace commandeered by al-Sistani sat at the far end. The only guards he could see were two in front of the ornate building. He would make his way closer to the island and then re-evaluate—

The steel barrel of a weapon pressed against the back of Oscar's head. A voice in a familiar tongue said, "Don't move or I'll kill you."

"You see," said a second voice, excited and less threatening. "I told you I saw something out here."

"Shut up. Let me handle this." The barrel nudged Oscar again. "Get up slowly with your hands above your head."

Oscar made a show of dropping the night-vision binoculars

in his left hand while he positioned the hunting knife in his right so it could not easily be seen. As instructed, he rose to his feet, his hands above his head.

"Now turn around slowly and face me."

Oscar complied. The gunman stood three feet away, his AK-47 automatic rifle aimed at Oscar's face. The excited man was a few paces to the gunman's right, his own weapon slung across his shoulder. He shone a flashlight onto Oscar's face. As the light played across his features, the man's voice trembled. "Allah has cursed us."

Even the gunman expressed a moment of hesitant shock, which cost him his life. Oscar twirled the hunting knife in his hand so he could use it as a weapon. He plunged the blade through the gunman's left temple, passed behind his eye, slicing through his middle cerebral artery, and puncturing the portions of the temporal lobe that control speech and motor function. The gunman went rigid and fouled himself. Oscar removed the knife and allowed the gunman to drop to the dirt where he silently hemorrhaged to death.

Coming out of his initial shock, the excited man reacted. Reaching up to his shoulder, he attempted to unsling his Kalashnikov. Oscar grabbed the strap and pulled the man into him. Gazing into Oscar's face, fear overcame the man. His mouth fell open to scream. Oscar couldn't allow that. That would bring the entire compound down upon him, and his target would live. Leaning forward, Oscar plunged his teeth into the man's throat around his Adam's apple and bit down. Yanking his head back, he tore away the skin and laryngeal cartilage, exposing the man's windpipe. The man called out, but the cry of terror and pain drowned in his own blood. Oscar released the man, who dropped to his knees and shook uncontrollably as his life flowed away. Clutching his hair in one hand, Oscar drove the blade through the man's temple, twisting in an arc to put a merciful end to his suffering. When the man went limp, Oscar lowered him to the dirt and removed the hunting knife from his skull.

Pausing long enough to ensure that his actions had not brought attention onto himself, Oscar stripped the gunman of his jacket and the excited man of his *shemagh* and frisked each body for anything that might be of use. He took only one of the AK-47s and any extra magazines they carried. Sliding the hunting knife back into its sheath, he removed his Makarov 9mm pistol from its holster and attached the suppressor, and then slid the weapon into the right pocket of the jacket. After slipping the corpses into the man-made lake, Oscar donned the clothing he had removed from them, draping the *shemagh* across his face to cover his features, and slung the Kalashnikov over his shoulder. Staying in the shadows as much as possible, he followed the lake away from the perimeter road, cut across a desolate area that had once been a lush garden, and approached the man-made island. The island measured only a quarter of a mile square, with an unguarded fifty-foot bridge providing the access point. Oscar made his way to it and crossed. The administrative and security buildings were between him and the palace.

The palace itself was more heavily protected, but still displayed an appalling lack of security for the ISIS leader, with only one guard visible along the front and left façades of the building. Oscar assumed single guards had been posted along the back and right side. The only exterior lights came from a chandelier that hung from the ceiling of the outer foyer, and even then, more than half the bulbs did not work. There were enough unlit spaces so that approaching the palace would be easy. He would make his way to the side of the palace, take out the guard, and sneak inside—

The guard standing duty in front of the palace noticed Oscar and kept a close eye on him as he drew closer, curious why someone would be approaching the palace so late at night. The guard had not readied his weapon, and so posed no immediate threat. Oscar altered his plans. If he headed for the side of the building, it would tip off the guard who would alert the others. Oscar would have to take out the guard and enter through the front door. With luck, the move would be brazen enough to pull off.

Reaching into his pocket for the Makarov, Oscar's fingers brushed against a pack of cigarettes and lighter. He immediately formed a plan for a diversion. Removing the pack, he pulled out a cigarette and placed it between his lips. Sliding the pack back inside his pocket, he took out the lighter. He bowed his head, flicked on the lighter, and placed it against the tip. The all-to-familiar action provided the perfect distraction, allowing him to approach to within twenty feet of the guard without having to acknowledge his presence. When Oscar raised his head, the guard gestured toward him.

"Do you have an extra one?"

Oscar nodded and slid his hand back inside his pocket, pretending to fumble around for the pack as he closed the distance. When within six feet, he removed the Makarov, aimed, and fired off three rounds before the guard could react. The 9mm rounds slammed into his chest, churning his heart and lungs into a gory mess, killing him instantly. Oscar leaned into the guard, propping him up momentarily so he could quietly slide him to the cement. The damage had already been done. Despite the suppressor, the guard along the left side of the palace had heard the muffled puffs of air. He called out to his friend.

"Ahmad, is every—"

Oscar fired two rounds into the guard's head as he turned the corner, dropping him instantly. The commotion alerted the palace. Yelling and the sound of running feet came from the other side of the front doors, followed by the klaxon of an alarm going off. Oscar popped the magazine from his Makarov, replaced it with a full one, and slid the firearm back into his pocket. Picking up the AK-47 from the dead guard, he checked to make sure the weapon was loaded and cocked, raised it into the high-ready position, and kicked open the front doors of the palace.

Five men raced across the foyer, stopping short at the sight of the intruder. One dropped his Kalashnikov, fell to his knees, and bowed his head against the floor, praying to Allah for mercy. Another turned and headed for the rear of the palace. Oscar fired a sustained burst, sweeping his weapon from side to side to eliminate the immediate threat from the other three guards. As they collapsed, he fired two rounds each into the kneeling guard and the one running away. Spinning around, Oscar closed the front doors to the palace and dropped the wooden beam across the supports, trapping himself—and his target—inside the building.

Several bursts of automatic fire came from above him. Bullets whizzed past, ricocheting off the doors and the sur-rounding jamb. Two hit their mark. Oscar felt one pass through his left shoulder and the other punch into his back. He could tell from the second impact that at least two ribs had been fractured. Spinning to his left and crouching behind a colonnade, Oscar assessed the situation.

Three guards were positioned at the top landing of the staircase to the right of the foyer. When he stuck his head out to observe, they fired again, continuing their barrage until Oscar heard the distinctive clicks signifying his attackers had expended their ammunition. The Kalashnikov he had taken from the guard outside was empty, so he unslung the one hanging on his shoulder, stepped out from behind the colon-nade, and fired back. The wound to his shoulder affected his aim, so his first shots were wide of their mark, forcing him to continue until the bolt of his Kalashnikov locked in the open position. Two guards were killed instantly with wounds to the chest and head, the latter splattering the wall behind him with blood and brain matter. The third took two bullets to the abdomen. He cried out and collapsed against the banister, clutching his midsection and grunting from pain.

Oscar raced up the stairs, heading for the room at the rear of the palace that he somehow knew housed al-Sistani. As he did, he released the empty magazine and tried to insert a new one. He had limited control over the movement in his left hand and could not get a grasp on the magazine. Oscar dropped the AK-47, reached into his pocket, and withdrew the Makarov. As he reached the top of the winding stairs, below him in the foyer he heard other guards pounding against the front doors. He had a few minutes at most to complete his mission.

Stepping over the bullet-riddled body of the two dead guards, Oscar headed down the hall.

As he neared the presidential suite, the heavy wooden door swung open and two women rushed out, the younger of the two naked except for a pair of black high heels. She held her hands above her head and yelled for him not to shoot. The second women wore a black *abaya*. She stayed behind the naked woman, her hands hidden in the folds of her robe-like garment. Oscar perceived the danger as the older woman rushed around her naked counterpart, raising a pump-action shotgun that she fired in his direction. Her aim was hurried and slightly off, yet at a range of less than ten feet more than a dozen buck shot tore into his chest and abdomen. He felt the projectiles rip their way through his body, most in the left lung and upper intestines. Those wounds would compromise his operational integrity within minutes. The old woman pumped another round into the shotgun's chamber. Before she could shoot again, Oscar leveled his Makarov and fired two rounds. Both bullets caught the older woman in the face, blasting away the right side of her head and lower jaw.

"You bastard!"

The naked woman rushed Oscar. She clutched at his face, hoping to gouge his eyes. Instead, she tore away his *shemagh* and exposed his face. She gasped and froze with fear. Oscar placed his partially-immobile left hand around the woman's throat and pushed her against one of the full-length mirrors that adorned each wall of the corridor. She did nothing to resist. Her eyes remained locked on his features, wide and glazed with terror. He smelled urine moments before he heard her pee hit the tiled floor. As he raised the Makarov to her forehead, her lips trembled and she stammered the question, "Wh-what the fuck are you?"

Oscar noticed his reflection in the mirror. He saw nothing out of the ordinary. Open lesions ran down the left side of his neck. Necrosis covered the left lower jaw and gums, having eaten away the flesh and muscles and giving that part of his face a skull-like visage. Cold emotionless eyes, like those of a shark, stared back at him.

What the fuck are you? he thought. *I'm the perfect killing machine.*

Oscar squeezed the trigger. The back of the naked woman's head erupted and the mirror shattered, erasing his reflection. He released his grip from around her neck, allowing her lifeless body to drop amongst the shards. An explosion echoed from the front foyer. The guards had gained access to the building. He had only seconds left. Pushing open the door to the presidential suite, he stepped inside.

A middle-aged man stood at the end of the oversized bed. He attempted to appear intimidating, an impossible task when naked and quivering like a frightened child. He clutched an AK-47 in his hands that he raised as Oscar entered, though from the way his hands shook, Oscar doubted he would be able to hit him even if he managed to pull the trigger. Oscar studied the man's features and assessed him with the deep-rooted memory he had of his target. The poorly-trimmed beard, more grey than black. The scraggily hair. The elongated nose. The three-inch-long scar that cut across his forehead. Oscar was face-to-face with al-Sistani, the man he had been ordered to assassinate.

From behind him, yelling and the sound of feet pounding up the stairs filled the corridor.

Oscar took several steps toward al-Sistani. The *shaykh*

dropped his weapon and raised his hands in front of him, hoping to buy the precious seconds needed for his bodyguards to arrive. "Wait. Allah is merciful. We can work out—"

Oscar raised his Makarov and fired two rounds into al-Sistani's chest. The *shaykh* fell backward onto the bed and slid to the floor, his blood smearing the white sheets crimson. His head rested against the edge of the mattress. He tried to speak but succeeded only in coughing, blood spurting out his mouth and down his chin. Oscar moved in front of the *shaykh* and placed the barrel of his Makarov against his forehead. The cleric nodded once, although Oscar was uncertain if from resignation of his fate or gratefulness that his suffering would soon end. Not that it mattered. Oscar squeezed the trigger repeatedly, emptying his last three rounds into al-Sistani's skull.

Automatic weapons fire erupted from the doorway as four bodyguards raced into the presidential suite and tried to stop the assassin. Oscar felt each round as it punched into his body. He would not be able to sustain such extensive damage for long. Turning to face his attackers, he stretched his arms out by his side to offer a better target. One-by-one his internal organs shut down. His breathing became labored and then stopped altogether as blood filled his lungs. His heart ceased functioning from a combination of internal damage and blood loss. His mind disengaged itself from the ravages his body endured, wandering back one final time to the woman with the olive skin and the child with the adoring eyes. For a moment, Oscar experienced a sensation he had not felt in ages—contentment. He closed his eyes and smiled at the fleeting thoughts before his body gave out and he passed into the beyond.

THE VITALS DISPLAY on the computer terminal flat lined, verifying Oscar had successfully completed his assignment and been terminated by external forces, just as Langley had anticipated.

Joel Chandy initiated the shutdown procedure. He had already remotely detonated the mini-helicopter over the Shatt al-Arab River three miles from the palace compound. With luck, the remnants would travel south with the current and eventually make their way to the Persian Gulf where they would never be seen again. Even if some of the pieces washed up along the banks or were picked up by a passing boat, it would be impossible to trace it back to the Agency. The mini-helicopter was an adaptation of the German-produced VC-100 Volocopter, although equipped with larger batteries to obtain greater distance and replacing the traditional twin blades with modulated spacing four-blade design to decrease noise emissions. DARPA had developed this military version of the Volocopter for this express purpose. Non-Official Cover (NOC) agents posing as European entrepreneurs had procured all the necessary parts over the course of several months through front companies in Europe and the Middle East. The mini-helicopter had been assembled by Agency engineers in a warehouse in northern Kuwait leased for the Americans by the British Embassy, and then infiltrated into the desert of the old Iran-Iraq War battlefields by an Army Special Forces team. All the parties concerned had been led to believe they were involved in developing an experimental device designed to infiltrate the airspace around suspected Iranian nuclear facilities to gather measurement and signature intelligence, or MASINT, on that nation's uranium enrichment efforts. The communication application Chandy used to control the mini-helicopter and receive the video feed from Oscar's bodycam had been covertly designed by DARPA precisely for this project; using a commercial communication application would have offered greater deniability, but at the risk that if the NSA had imbedded tracking code on the application they might be able to pick up the signal and begin asking unwanted questions. He could only be detected through a government service triangulating his position, but Chandy made certain he would not be around long enough for anyone to locate and dispatch someone.

The same attention to detail had gone into the denial and deception campaign associated with Oscar. Everything, from his clothing and hunting knife to the insulin pump used to control his medication and the mini-body camera attached to his headband, had been purchased with cash from local shops in Dubai and Abu Dhabi. A half-way decent forensics investigation of Oscar's body would uncover his origins, but that would open up a can of worms for Iran, not the United States. Since less than ten people were briefed on the full extent of the operation, himself included, this came as close as possible to being the perfect covert operation.

Chandy typed in the command to initiate the self-erase program on his terminal's hard drive and issued the order to shut down. The next time he powered up, the program would demand the user enter a specialized twelve-character passcode within fifteen seconds. If that failed to happen, a degaussing wand built into the laptop would activate and the magnetic charge would reset the hard drive to its original settings, permanently eliminating all stored data and applications, making it impossible for technical forensics to retrieve any of it.

As his computer shut down, Chandy checked his work area to ensure he had loaded everything in his backpack he had brought with him. He did not want to leave behind any indications of his presence here.

Here referred to Camp Liberty, one of many bases erected by the CIA along the Kuwait-Iraq border in the months prior to Operation Iraqi Freedom. At the time, these camps were used as forward-deployed bases for those Agency personnel who would infiltrate Iraq ahead of the Allied ground forces. Following the conclusion of hostilities, the camps were used to ferry supplies into the occupied territory until they were eventually abandoned and left for the desert to reclaim. It took him several days to find one still usable that had not already been taken over by the locals. He thought it fitting that Camp Liberty had provided one final, vital service against America's enemies.

The computer screen went blank, and the green power light switched off. Chandy closed the casing, slid the computer into its carry case, and zipped it closed. Slinging the backpack over his left shoulder and taking the computer case in the same hand, he made his way across the main building and outside into the cold desert night. Off to the east, the first rays of sunshine tinted the horizon yellowish-orange. With luck, he could make the two-hour drive and reach the heart of Kuwait City before rush hour traffic became too heavy. First, he would stop by the strip mall down the street from the American Embassy compound and send an encrypted text via a pre-paid disposable cell phone to his boss in northern Virginia informing him he would be returning home tomorrow, the signal that the Oscar mission had been a success. He would then return to his hotel and sleep before catching a flight back to the States later that evening.

Opening the door of his Land Rover, he placed the two cases on the floor in front of the passenger seat and climbed behind the wheel. Pulling away from Camp Liberty, Chandy headed out across the desert, his mind thinking about a warm meal and a hot shower rather than the assassin he had sent to his death.

A Thank You to My Readers

I know I say this in every novel, but it's the truth. In addition to working for the CIA, writing has been one of the two most fulfilling things I've done with my life. The best part is having fans who read my books, enjoy them, and want more. I'm incredibly fortunate and grateful to have such a loyal fan base. You keep reading and I'll keep writing.

If you enjoyed *The Ghosts of the Bethlehem Asylum*, please post a review on Amazon and/or Goodreads. Reviews drive the algorithms that get a writer's books more exposure on Amazon. It doesn't have to be long—just a rating and a sentence or two about why you liked or disliked it. To be successful in this genre, I need your support. Also, tell your friends about the book and post your review on Scott Baker's Realm of Zombies, Monsters, and the Paranormal.

Be sure to read *The Ghosts of Eden Hollow*, *The Ghosts of Salem Village*, and *The Ghosts the Maria Doria*, the first three novels in the Tatyana paranormal saga.

Thank you all in advance.

Acknowledgments

Non-writers think writing is hard. It's actually fun. The difficult part is the editing, making certain the details are accurate, and publishing. It's a complicated process involving many people, all of whom deserve to be recognized.

A huge debt of gratitude goes to Rhian Lockard. When I started researching *The Ghosts of Eden Hollow*, I had little understanding of the paranormal. Rhian spent an hour with me on the phone one evening explaining the reality of spiritual hauntings and spectral cleansings and answering all my questions. That background has been instrumental in writing these books. She's been extremely supportive. However, any errors in how to perform a cleansing, or any intentional diversions from reality for the sake of literary license (such as allowing spectral images to adopt corporeal form or mentally merging with a living person) are all on me.

A major thanks go out to my beta readers who have been with me from book one, Dan Uebel and Doc Fried. They pointed out grammatical/spelling errors, plot flaws, and inconsistencies and offered their opinion on whether they liked the story. I would be lost without them.

Warren Design created the cover art for this book as well as the others in the Tatyana paranormal series. Their work perfectly fits the mood of this book. I'm looking forward to working with them in the future.

About the Author

Scott M. Baker was born and raised in Everett, Massachusetts, and spent twenty-three years in northern Virginia working for the Central Intelligence Agency and traveling through Europe, Asia, and the Middle East. Scott is now retired and lives outside of Salem, New Hampshire, with his Bassett/Beagle mix Fred and two cats who treat him as their human servant.

In addition to his paranormal series, he is currently writing the *Nurse Alissa vs. the Zombies* and *The Chronicles of Paul* sagas, his latest zombie apocalypse series. Previous works include *Operation Majestic*, his Nazi time travel novel (think *Raiders of the Lost Ark* meets *Back to the Future* – with aliens); *Frozen World*, his stand-alone post-apocalyptic novel; the *Shattered World* series, his five-book young adult post-apocalypse thriller about a group of adventurers attempting to close interdimensional portals into Hell; *The Vampire Hunters* trilogy, about humans fighting the undead in Washington D.C.; *Rotter World*, *Rotter Nation*, and *Rotter Apocalypse*, his first post-apocalyptic zombie saga; *Yeitso*, his homage to the giant monster movies of the 1950s that he loved watching as a kid; as well as several zombie-themed novellas and anthologies.

Please check out Scott's social media accounts for the latest information on future books, upcoming events, and other fun stuff.

Facebook: Scott Baker's Realm of Zombies, Monsters,
and the Paranormal:
facebook.com/groups/1162724727634526

Twitter:
twitter.com/vampire_hunters

YouTube:
youtube.com/channel/UC5AyCVrEAncr2E0N5XoyUdg/pla
ylists

Instagram:
instagram.com/scottmbakerwriter

TikTok:
tiktok.com/@authorscottmbaker

Blog:
scottmbakerauthor.blogspot.com

Wyrd Realities Homepage:
www.wyrdrealities.net/